SAYING GOODBYE

written by

SHELLI SHEREE

Originally published by Shelli Sheree
First Published December 2020

Cover Photograph by Billie Reed
Cover Design by Sheree Publishing
Interior Design by Sheree Publishing

Printed in the United States of America

ISBN: 978-1-7363538-1-3
Library of Congress Control Number: 2018675309

Sheree
Publishing

Dedicated to my daughter,
who survived the summer of 2016

CONTENTS

Dedicated to my daughter,
who survived the summer of 2016

CONTENTS

PROLOGUE

I never thought this is how I would have to say goodbye to my parents. I always expected life to go on as planned. After college, I would begin a career, marry, and eventually have children. Vacations and holidays would be spent with family. Weekly phone calls to my mom and dad, frequent visits, and a home full of love and laughter would suffice. I don't need fancy clothes or jewelry or a fifty thousand dollar car. I could live a simple life as long as it was with someone who loved me.

Now I sit, with a thousand thoughts whirling through my mind, not even knowing how to begin. I don't know how my life got so tangled up into a web of mysteries. I have been given one last chance to say goodbye to my parents. Who, in his right mind, tells someone that she has one last chance to say goodbye to her parents? It would be nice if I could just call them or call my sister right now, but phone calls are not an option. At what point did my life fall apart? Just seven months ago I experienced my worst nightmare, one that no wife would ever want to encounter, and now here I am experiencing another.

I thought Wednesday, September 17th had been the most wretched day of my life, but yesterday was even worse. I have been given a thirty-six hour window to say goodbye. I am so confused. I can't believe this is happening to me. I'm at a beach house confined to a second

1

floor bedroom with nowhere to go. I'm trapped inside this house. I am confused. My captors are actually treating me with dignity and respect. I don't understand. This is nothing like the movies when someone is brutally beaten and tortured awaiting ransom. I've been given plenty of food, water, soda, meals, and snacks.

Better yet is the view. I actually have a view of the ocean with the sound of every wave crashing into the soft sand. Unfortunately, my window is nailed shut so I can't enjoy the breeze that comes along with the fascination of sand and water. I actually think I might be in Texas on the Gulf of Mexico near South Padre Island, but I don't know for sure. I might even be near Flagler Beach in Florida. I am trying to remember what the sand is like in Florida. I know it changes from southern Florida to northern Florida and the Gulf side is completely different than the Atlantic side, but I haven't been there in years. My memory eludes me.

I must have been brought here last night. I don't remember anything. I woke to the sound of the waves crashing onto the beach. The sun had just risen slightly above the horizon when I woke up. I always wake at the crack of dawn, but something was different today. I have a horrible headache and I feel groggy. On my first attempt, I struggled to keep my eyes open and fell back to sleep. Now that I am awake, I keep yawning. I just don't feel like my normal self right now. My eyes are heavy. It's the same feeling I get when I am awakened too early from a heavy sleep.

A plate of scrambled eggs, bacon, and raisin bread with

real butter sat on a tray next to my bed. A white mug filled to the brim with apple juice and a pinch of caramel, topped with whipped cream accompanied the meal along with a clear eight ounce glass of ice water with lemon and a small stem juice glass with orange juice. Two small, elongated pills were on the tray next to the water. When I picked them up to observe, the microscopic print read Motrin. My kidnappers obviously knew I must have been experiencing a headache now. I have no idea when the breakfast arrived, but it's here and it is still warm.

There are only two people who know how much I like a Caramel Penlight, my sister, Rachel and my husband, Calvin. Several years ago, after Rachel's youngest child, Claire, was in kindergarten, she and her husband decided to open a small coffee shop in Racine, Wisconsin. My sister is a coffee connoisseur. She named it, Penguins Plus. When Claire was a toddler she used to pretend that she was a penguin all the time. If you asked her what she wanted to be when she grew up, she would say a penguin. Rachel thought the name would be clever for her business since people could relate to the icy Wisconsin winters just like the penguins living in the icy waters of the Antarctica. I jokingly told my sister that I wanted a Carmel Penlight one day, rather than a Caramel Delight. The name stuck.

The strange thing about this choice of beverage is simple. I never drink hot drinks in warm weather. Both Rachel and Calvin know that I only drink hot drinks in cold weather, which means I only order this drink when I visit my sister. Why would anyone serve a hot caramel drink instead of coffee? When I felt the crystal clear glass of the window while trying to open one, it was warm to the touch, another obvious indication that I am further south than north.

My room was rather nice. It had soft green walls with white trim. A king size bed with wicker head and footboards faced the water. In one corner of the room next to the window was an upholstered lounge chair, and in the other corner was a wicker rocking chair. A solid green seat cushion with a floral pillow matched the colors of the large striped bed linens. They were green, light blue, orange, and brown. A round wicker nightstand was on the far side of the bed, and on the near side stood a single drawer white night stand. Along the inside wall near the bathroom was a desk and chair.

There were two large pieces of black-and-white art framed. One was a field of sunflowers, and the other was a row of twenty mailboxes all lined up one after another along a dirt road with nothing, but barren land and tumble weed in the background. The sunflowers reminded me of a place in Minnesota that I had driven by several times as a child on my way to camp. The other photo easily could have been taken in New Mexico or Arizona. It definitely had a southwest flare that was completely different than the Midwest.

Next to the tray on the night stand was a note, plain white copy paper, a package of three new black marking pens, and two plain white envelopes. The instructions, typed on the note, were simple.

You have thirty-six hours from now to draft a farewell letter to your parents. You will not be seeing them again. If you say anything about your location or how you got here, there will be consequences. Put their address on the envelope, and your return address. Do not seal the envelope. If you choose to cooperate, you will be reunited with your husband.

I almost fell out of bed when I read the note. Cal is alive. He's alive, I thought. I would have screamed out loud, but my head hurt too badly. I picked up the paper a second time and read the note again. Then I looked at the supplies on the table. Even in my excitement to learn that I might be able to see Cal again, I noticed another strange thing. There were two envelopes rather than one. I am rather confident that I know my parent's address, and I would not make the mistake of addressing someone else. I'm not sure why there would be two envelopes when I am only allowed to write one letter. That seemed odd to me.

I contemplated whether or not I should eat the breakfast. It looked good, and it smelled even better. Could I trust that it was safe? There is no doubt that I had been kidnapped, and now I was expected to trust my kidnappers. I was hoping it wasn't a trick. I decided that it probably wasn't or they would not have given me instructions to write a letter. My hunger got the best of me. I ate the food and drank the juice. I felt a little stronger within a half hour. I did not drink the Caramel Penlight, and I decided to wait to drink the water. I definitely might need the pain relief for my pounding headache.

Despite my effort not to take the Motrin, I could only hold out for an hour. My head was still pounding, and I knew I needed some relief to carry out the task at hand. I desperately tried to stop crying, but the gravity of my situation was over-whelming dismal. I was riding a roller coaster of emotions. I was adrenalized by the thought of seeing Calvin again, but very distraught about the letter to my parents. The more I cried, the worse my head ached. I finally decided to take one pill to see if that would help. I needed to be able to think clearly if I was going to write this letter. I also needed to focus to see if there was anyway out of this mess.

How could I have ever gotten myself into a situation like this? What did I do wrong? Who is doing this to me? Why do I have to say goodbye to my parents? I just want my normal, ev-eryday- sometimes boring- life back. After lying on the bed for another half hour rolled up in a ball of tears, I firmly placed my feet on the floor and began to pace back and forth across the room for several minutes, before I settled down on the lounge chair in front of the window. I was hoping to see somebody who could help or something that would give me a clue to my whereabouts. There was nothing except complete tranquility along with the rhythm of waves.

It then occurred to me that I should search the entire room for cameras, microphones, and any another hidden de-vice or gadget that allowed my captors to watch me. I looked into every piece of furniture, every nook and cranny, and art-work without finding a thing. After searching intently for thirty-five minutes, I gave up. I couldn't find a thing. I was exhausted and my head still hurt. Maybe a shower would help. I always found something exhilarating about beads of water flowing gently onto my head and shoulders. I desperately needed to wake up. If it couldn't be from the nightmare I was dreaming, then to face the day and task at hand.

The private attached bathroom was clean. Two hand towels hung on a towel bar directly across from the door next to the sink. One had an embroidered yellow pineapple centered in the middle and the other a parrot. Unlike most hotel rooms, this bathroom had a walk-in shower. The shower had large tiles with three rows of smaller accent tiles throughout the middle of the shower. The middle row of tile was a mirror image of the hand towels with pineapples and parrots alternating each tile. Someone took the time to coordinate this matching detail. I liked it.

I quietly picked up the desk chair and carried it in to the bathroom with me. I turned on the light and fan, and locked the door behind me. I then jammed the back of the chair underneath the door handle with the legs crammed against the bowl of the toilet. At this point in time, I still couldn't trust anyone and felt the need for any additional security that could possibly protect me. Even if someone could unlock the door, it would be difficult for him to enter. The chair gave me added peace of mind as I pulled my shirt over my head waiting for the water to warm to the perfect temperature.

A white robe hung on a hanger while white bath towels were neatly folded on the shelf with new bottles of shampoo and conditioner. I didn't notice any clean clothes in the drawers when I searched for cameras earlier. I would have to put my own clothes back on. They smelled. Then I remembered. I had been riding my bike at the time of the incident. That must have been the last thing I was doing. I definitely needed to wash my clothes. I guess the robe could work for a few hours while my riding clothes dried.

I used the coconut scented shampoo to hand wash my clothes while I showered. I then wrung my clothes out and hung them on the towel bar in the back of the shower to dry. The odor was gone now. My shower was refreshing and peaceful. Unfortunately, I couldn't quite relax thinking that an intruder could try to barge in at any time. I quickly slid into the bathrobe then placed my hair up in the towel to dry. That didn't last long. The towel was heavy on my head and only made my head hurt again. I opened every drawer and cabinet, but did not find a hair dryer. I would have to let my hair air-dry. No one entered the bathroom, giving me an ounce of comfort that the guys' intentions were not to harm me.

Lunch, on the other hand, arrived while I was taking the shower. I'm not sure whether this was intentional or not. I'm sure anyone who listened could hear the sound of the water running in the shower. It must have arrived around noon. The sun was high in the sky and the shadows of the house and several palm trees fell directly beneath them when I looked outside again. I could always tell the time of day by the shadows produced by the sun, a skill I learned as a kid.

It seemed like I had just eaten breakfast, but now wasn't the time to complain that the meal came sooner than I wished. A turkey sandwich on multigrain bread was served with Muenster cheese, lettuce, and mayonnaise. I actually prefer miracle whip more so than mayonnaise, but was thankful that the sandwich was delicious. Sweet potato chips, chocolate chip cookies, white milk and ice water with lemon were also served. I really wasn't hungry, but ate anyway. I wasn't sure if I would continue to be fed or not. Nourishment might be a key to my survival. Every bite of the chips echoed in my mind as I sat wondering, waiting, and wishing. With each crunch, the agonizing thought of saying goodbye felt like a jackhammer being drilled down into the depths of my soul. My head was still aching, so I took the last pill when I finished the lunch.

After eating, I felt better prepared to switch my attention to the letter and its requirements. My time was running out. The clock was ticking. My thirty-six hour window was dwindling down quickly. I sat down at the desk to write. "My parents or my husband?" I thought. This wasn't just about saying goodbye to my parents. This was about making a choice between the people I loved the most. What if I chose not to write the letter? And, if I did write it, would that mean I was saying hello to a new life? I had so many questions, but very few answers.

Chapter One
HIS STEPS

Racine, Wisconsin, is a small town on Lake Michigan just a short drive from the Illinois border. My dad, who has since retired, was heavily involved in the revitalization of the Racine lakefront that now embraces a 920-slip marina. It was here where I spent most of my summer days growing up. I loved the water, and I loved to sail. I started working at the marina when I was only twelve years old, cleaning boats and helping out where ever I could. In return, I always found someone to take me sailing. It's there, out on the open waters, that I found peace and serenity. I lived just about a mile from the docks, so every morning in the summer my sister and I would ride our bikes down to the lake to watch the sun rise. Everybody loved us there. We never worried about breakfast or lunch because we knew someone would always feed us. Everyone in town knew our parents. Our dad, Michael, was a local architect. Our mom, Elizabeth, was a registered nurse who worked in a nearby nursing home. No one ever called her Elizabeth though. Her nickname was Sweetie. I have no idea who gave her that name, but it stuck.

Rachel, was just a year older than me. She met her husband in college, married after they graduated, and in a few short years began a family. She has three boys and a daughter. I went to Robert Morris University in Chicago and studied drafting and design. I actually thought I would follow in the footsteps of my father by becoming an architect. Those plans changed quickly upon graduation. I was given the opportunity to do a year internship for Albuquerque Studios designing sets for their movies. I fell in love with the movie industry, and after my year stint was offered a full time job working for the Studio.

Since sailing isn't easily accomplished here in New Mexico, I bought a mountain bike in hopes of finding a new hobby. Whenever anyone asks, I tell them that I really miss the water and my family, but biking here in the mountains reminds me of Lake Michigan. Everyone typically gives me a funny look when I say that the mountains remind me of water. Once I am high above the city, I can look for miles and see nothing more than desert, just like looking across Lake Michigan and seeing nothing more than water. It's that sense of tranquility that keeps bringing me back out on my bike just like the water drew me near when I was young.

My husband, Calvin, is also an avid mountain bike enthusiast. We met in the local bike club that we both belong. When we first met, we only lived a block away from each other. Cal is an entrepreneur, who, like so many others here in Albuquerque, owns a hot air balloon business, Striking High. There are a lot of hot air balloon businesses here in town that provide rides for tourism. Cal's business, unlike most, is a manufacturing company that makes hot air balloons. Even though he takes a lot of people out on rides, he does it on third and fourth test rides. Each and every balloon that his business manufacturers is tested four or five times in air to pass its safety inspection. Between his career and mine, we have been having the time of our lives.

It has already been ten years since we said our "I do's." It was just a few weeks ago after we celebrated our 10th anniversary that we re-evaluated our priorities. We both want to have a family, but have been enjoying our careers so much that we haven't committed to a drastic lifestyle change. In all fairness to Cal, it was me who feared making the commitment. Although I knew Cal would be a great father, I didn't want someone else raising our kids. I also thought I should be a stay at home mom until the kids entered school. I am thirty-three years old now and there is no better time than now to begin our family. At least, that is what I thought just a few short months ago. Yet, life threw a curve ball that I could never have dreamt. A perfectly normal morning turned into a nightmare that seemed like it lasted for three years. It really only lasted several months, but when I finally thought I had found a new routine to my life, a new nightmare began, leaving me in a quandary once again.

Cal and I got up every morning at sunrise. He would leave the house around 6:00 am every Monday, Wednesday, and Friday morning to lift weights and train at a nearby gym. On Tuesdays and Thursday mornings, we typically would go for an hour-long bike ride before we started our day. It was on a Wednesday that my life changed unexpectedly. Cal ran to the gym like he always did, just a mile and a half away from our home. He typically works out for an hour, showers, grabs a cappuccino and muffin next door at Starbucks and walks a half mile to his office, an old brick building that he had converted into the warehouse work shop that he uses to build the balloons. Not only was it convenient and inexpensive, but it was large enough to house his multiple balloon projects.

It was 9:38 am when I received a text message from Cal's assistant, Ann, asking why Cal had not shown up to work yet. She had tried calling and texting him multiple times with no response. I was surprised. I was on location of a new movie being shot on the outskirts of town near Shooting Range State Park. I stopped dead in my tracks and called her immediately.

"Ann," I said, "Cal left for the gym around 6:00 this morning like he always does." No one has seen or heard from him since?" I asked.

"No," she responded.

"I will call the gym to see if he clocked in there. They should be able to give me some answers," I told Ann as I hung up in disbelief.

"Hi Rob. This is Caroline Richards," I said when Rob finished his telephone greeting. "Did Cal show up at the gym this morning?"

"Yea, Caroline, on time as usual. He showered, and clocked out at 7:44 am, said he was stopping by Starbucks and would see me on Friday. Is everything okay?" he asked.

"I think so, Rob, I was just wondering. Thanks so much for your help," I said as I quickly hung up to call Starbucks.

"Hi Susie, it's me, Caroline," I said when Susie answered the phone. Cal and I always stopped at the same Starbucks each morning. I would arrive a few minutes earlier than him each day because it was a little further to work for me. Being on a new set today, I opted to get coffee at work this morning. "Did Cal stop in this morning?" I asked.

"Yep, on time as usual. It was 7:45 on the dot. I had his

cappuccino and muffin waiting for him," she told me.

"Great. Thanks Susie. I'll see you tomorrow," I said not ever thinking that my tomorrow might be flipped up side down.

"Ann, it's me," I said when I called Cal's assistant back. "Cal worked out at Planet Fitness, then stopped by Starbucks. He told both Rob and Susie that he was heading to work. Maybe he had an errand to go on, and it's taking him a little longer since he walked today," I explained trying to reassure Ann and myself that everything was fine.

"Okay, just let me know if you hear anything else," Ann said as she hung up.

I immediately called Cal when I got off the phone, but was sent directly to his voicemail. That was odd. He never sends me to his voicemail, I thought.

I tried to get back to work and stay focused on the shoot, but it didn't take long for my boss, Christopher, the production manager, to sense that something was wrong. I explained the odd phone call that I had received and the lack of response from Cal. He assured me that everything was probably fine, but told me to take a long lunch break. I had a crew of five people who assist me, and an intern. I handed by clipboard over to my assistant, and told him that I would be back in a while. I didn't tell anyone else at work what had happened earlier because at this point I did not want to be over reacting.

I climbed into my Land Rover with my dog, Lucy, at my side. Lucy was a completely black dog that I had rescued two years previously from a shelter. She was a Labrador/Border Collie mix. She followed me everywhere I went. She was the best dog ever. She never barked and was friendly with everyone she met. This morning, even Lucy could sense that I was distraught. She whimpered, and laid her nose down on my lap as we drove away. On most days, her nose was out the window catching the warm breeze against her face.

Now I needed a game plan. I guess I didn't have one when I got into the truck. I had already driven a half-mile down the road, and needed to decide which fork in the road to take. I quickly thought to myself what was the most logical step. First, I would stop by Cal's office. I could easily drive by it before heading home. Maybe he was sick and had gone home, but failed to tell anyone. He easily could have turned off his phone, and forgot to turn it back on. That sounded more like the Cal I knew. Feeling good about my explanation, I turned on the radio rather loud and drove with a new purpose. I led myself to believe the lie my conscious was sharing. Calvin was fine, and I was just making a big deal over nothing. Cal probably had a surprise for me, and I was going to ruin it by coming home from work early to check on him.

It took me around thirty minutes to arrive at his office. When I walked in, I knew immediately that everyone else was concerned too. I could hear a pin drop if I would take the time to listen. The radio was turned off, something that never happened unless they were in an all staff meeting which took place every Monday morning. His crew consisted of five office personnel including a controller, five design experts, and twenty production staff. I walked straight into Ann's office where she sat along with Kevin, the controller, and Drew, the production chief. I could tell by the looks on their faces that no one had heard or seen Cal yet today.

"Could he be in a meeting?" I asked when I walked through the door.

"I don't think so," Ann replied. "He doesn't have one listed on his calendar for today.

"Could he be meeting with a local supplier?" I suggested.

Drew responded to this question. "No, I don't think so Caroline. We met with Anthony yesterday, and George last week. I can't think of anyone else we would need to see anytime soon."

I had just convinced myself on the way over that Cal was home sick, and then I walked in here asking questions. My plan had already backfired before I even had time to check it out. "Well," I said, "Maybe he wasn't feeling well and decided to go back home. I'll go home to see if he is there and give you a call in a few minutes. Just keep working and I'm sure everything will be okay. I'll let you know as soon as I get home.

Lucy and I piled back into the truck and then sped away. It literally took me about three minutes to drive home because I didn't have any red lights. I jumped out of the truck with Lucy at my feet, and ran into the house. We never locked our door so it was easy to run right in. I'm not sure why we would lock it, yet I really didn't have a good reason why we shouldn't either.

"Cal, Cal," I called out as I ran through the living room, up the stairs, and into our bedroom. I was expecting him to talk back to me after awakening him from his nap, but to my surprise there was complete silence as I turned the corner into our room. The bed was made pristinely as we had left it when we awoke this morning. The very first thing we did every morning was to make our bed when we got up. It took about two seconds with each of us grabbing the covers from our own side. It was quick, easy, and always made coming to bed at night a little more comfortable and appealing.

I walked from room to room calling Cal's name with Lucy trailing by my feet. The air was filled with silence. Each breath I took felt full like the dense, dripping humidity that I remember feeling on days when we visited my cousins who lived in Indiana when I was growing up. The air was so thick that it was hard to breath. I knew it had to be me and not the air. Albuquerque didn't have that kind of air, ever.

I slumped onto the soft, opulent rug resting my back against the sofa when I returned to the living room. I had just searched every room in the house with no signs of my husband's return. I came up empty. I honestly expected Calvin to be home. I had convinced myself that he was home sick. The tears began to roll down my warm cheeks as I cuddled with Lucy. This couldn't be happening.

"Now what do I do Lucy? I asked. "Papa is gone. He's missing. No one knows where he is right now," I told my four-legged friend. My subconscious kept saying that there had to be a logical reason, and that Calvin was fine. My gut told me a different story. I sat with Lucy crying for ten minutes when the phone startled me. I jumped to my feet and ran into the kitchen to see who was calling. I don't even know why we have a landline anymore. No one ever seems to use it. I think our cable package was cheaper having a landline than not having one, so on rare occasion I would use it or Cal would fax with it.

I immediately looked at the caller I.D. My heart sunk

17

again. It was an 800 number. You know the type. The one that always has a solicitor at the other end. I didn't even pick it up. I just let it ring as I ran back into the living room and flung myself onto the sofa. I laid there for another six or seven minutes before a new plan entered my head.

Maybe I should go to Starbucks and ask to see their video monitor. We were good friends with everyone who worked there, and the owner was a dear friend who rode bikes with us several times a month. "Come on, Lucy," I shouted as I ran back out of the house towards our truck. "Jump in girl," I demanded. I forgot to call Ann back to tell her that Cal was not home.

"Hey Susie, is Peter around?" I asked on my way in when I dodged an older woman who was walking out.

"He sure is," she responded. "He's in the back room. Everything okay?" she then asked.

"I hope so Susie. I really hope so," I assured myself.

"Hey Peter," I said as I peaked through the door. "Can I talk to you for a minute?" I asked.

"Of course, you can Caroline. What's up?" he asked.

I explained what had transpired over the past four and a half hours. "Is there anyway I can review your security tapes to see if anything suspicious can be found? Maybe Cal walked the opposite way down the street. Or maybe we can see a car pull up. I'm just looking for anything that might give me a clue as to his whereabouts."

"Oh, dear," Peter responded. "I might be able to help, but I'm not sure how much. My cameras inside the cafe are working perfectly fine, but I've been having problems with my outside camera. When the storm blew through here several weeks ago, my camera was hit with some shingles that blew off the roof of this place. We can check it though."

Peter and I spent the next half hour reviewing footage from earlier that day. Everything and everybody seemed normal. Peter was his bubbly self when he approached the counter to get his coffee from Susie. He spoke with her for a minute, paid with cash, left a tip, and walked out the front door. No one followed him out, and he appeared to go in the direction of his office.

We looked for strangers or people who appeared apprehensive, but found nothing out of the ordinary. Most of the customers were people that Peter knew. Most of his morning customers were locals who stopped daily. Today, there were several new faces that Peter did not recognize, but they ordered coffee, paid, and walked back out like everyone else. There was an elderly couple that came in just a few minutes before Cal walked in the front door. They ordered two coffees and a bagel, and proceeded to sit down at a small table that viewed the street. They stayed for almost twenty minutes before they stood up to leave. Cal had been long gone by this point.

Next to the coffee shop was a small bookstore that featured historical references about Old Historic Nob Hill and some of the local tribes that once occupied this region. It looked like it was built out of sticks, and if the wind blew hard enough it would tumble down. There is no way it had any security cameras at all. It had a single bolt lock.

The barbershop that Cal used was next to the bookstore. It had bright neon lights that everyone could see from a mile away. It had been remodeled a number of years ago to better fit in with the rest of the neighborhood, but it too had seen better days. There were a few younger guys working there now, but Cal's favorite barber was Mr. Boots. He was probably seventy by now. I had never met anyone who could make Cal laugh the way Mr. Boots could. They would entertain each other for hours with their jokes. There was no high tech security there either, just Mr. Boots' old dog, Rascal. If he liked you, he would lift his head long enough to make eye contact. If he didn't like you, then he would slowly stand up, sniff all around your feet, and then try to leave a puddle on top of your shoe. No lie. I've seen this dog turn several strangers around, screaming at the top of their lungs as they exited the shop without a haircut.

A small art gallery that features pottery and bright colored originals was three doors down. It was a newer building and had a camera at every door. Once a month, new artists were featured and we often found ourselves sipping a glass of wine at one of their debuts.

Peter told me that he would check with each of these stores to see if the cameras at the art gallery caught anything unusual. None of them were even open when Cal stopped by Starbucks. He would also make a few phone calls to his buddies down the street. One owned an authentic Mexican restaurant across the street three blocks down, and the other had a dentist office.

At this point, I didn't know what to think or do. I knew I shouldn't worry because Cal was probably all right. Maybe he had the ultimate birthday surprise for me that he was handling today. My birthday was four weeks out, but maybe he was thinking ahead. I wasn't sure if I should go back to work or go home and wait. As I pulled away from Starbucks, I stopped at the stop sign and turned the car around. I had a new plan. I would walk the route that Cal would have taken if he had gone to work. It was less than three quarters of a mile from here to his office. I could easily walk that and back in twenty minutes. I pulled back into the parking spot, threw my purse into the back seat under a blanket, grabbed by keys and phone and began my little trot.

The noon sun was high overhead now and shadows at a minimal. I looked for signs everywhere. Maybe I could find a fragment of his t-shirt, his phone, or Starbucks coffee cup thrown into an ally. I was looking for anything that looked astray. An overturned garbage can or the dreaded stain on the sidewalk would have caught my attention this afternoon. I didn't see a thing. My mind was still turning, and I was hot. The temperature had already soared to ninety-five degrees. I was afraid if I turned my head in the wrong direction that I might miss something.

I continued to look when I approached the local bike club that we belonged. I opened the door that swung to the left. With all the bikes that go in and out of this shop, it struck me funny this time that the door swung to the left. Why wasn't there a sliding door, an automatic door? A door that was hands free would make it easier for people to walk in and out with a bicycle in tow. As soon as I walked in I heard my name, Caroline, being called from the back corner of the store.

Are we still planning to hit the North Foothills in the morning," Joshua asked. As soon as I walked close enough for him to see me up close, he knew something was wrong. "Caroline, what is it?" he asked.

"Well, I'm not really sure," I said as I motioned for him to come to the back room. I immediately sat down on the wooden stool next to a bike stand that held a Trek in place. "Cal is missing," I told him trying to hold back the tears. "He didn't show up for work this morning. I'm just walking his usual route to work. He worked out at Planet Fitness this morning, then stopped at Starbucks like he does every day. He told Susie that he was headed to work as usual. Peter and I reviewed his security tape, and everything seems perfectly normal. He left with his coffee in hand and headed down this way. Did you happen to see him walk by?" I asked.

"Jason and I were just coming back from an early morning ride. We were around the corner about a block away on the other side of Sixty-Six when we saw him in front of the 66 Diner. Looked to me like he was headed to his shop," Joshua commented. I'll ask around to see if anyone else saw him.

"Right now, it sounds like you and Jason were the last to see him, and he was only a half a block from the office. Well, thanks for the information. I'm heading that way now. Please let me know if you see him or hear anything else," I said as I turned to walk back to the front of the store.

"Hey, Caroline, just call me if you need anything else. I'm sure Cal will show up this afternoon yet," he assured.

"I'll let you know," I said as I walked out the front door. Joshua loved owning a shop here near the strip. I had known him longer than Cal. He was a trusted friend who introduced the two of us years ago when I first moved here. I knew I could rely on him any time of day.

Traffic was starting to pick up now. The neon lights that

showered this area at night were still asleep. This was a nightlife community, a nostalgic one near the infamous Route 66. Many locals stay in their cocoons during the mornings before appearing with new wings just before twelve. Once noon strikes, the day is in full swing around these parts. I decided to stop at the diner. I ordered a chicken sandwich and bought a soda fountain drink to go. I knew no one would have seen Cal this morning because the diner is only opened for breakfast on the weekends. I just sat in the restaurant for a few minutes watching people come and go, unconcerned about the troubles of my day. Nothing seemed out of place.

Two blocks down the street was Striking High. I walked back into the old warehouse only long enough to hear that Cal still had not shown up. I tried to keep my composure and told the few staff members that I saw that Cal probably had a meeting that he had forgotten to mark on the calendar. I retraced my steps and headed back to Starbucks. I was mentally and emotionally exhausted. I knew there was no way I could go back to work this afternoon. As I sat in my truck, waiting for the air conditioner to kick in, I quickly texted my boss to say that I would need to take the remainder of the day off. My crew was completely ready for the shoot today, so I knew they would be able to get along without me.

Chapter Two
THE INVASION

About a mile from Cal's office is the local police station. I had driven by many times before, but never had a reason to stop until today. I intentionally drove there on my way back home and parked on the street in front of the building. I sat still, numb from the possibility of what might have happened to my husband. I wanted desperately to walk inside, give a report, and allow the police to take over the investigation. I had done everything I could at this point. I didn't know what else to do. They could access all the security monitors in the area. Surely someone must have seen him disappear off the street just a half a block from his office. My thoughts told me that the police would laugh at my story. My husband had only been missing about five hours now. According to their definition of missing, he wouldn't be missing at all. I could already hear them say that he just had another place to be or an errand to run, but forgot to tell anyone about it. I knew that was a logical explanation, even though it wouldn't be the one I wanted to hear.

After crying for a few more minutes, my head began to throb. "Take a deep breath," I told myself. "Breath in, breath out," I whispered. "Get a hold of yourself, Caroline," I said out loud. I then noticed that my fingers were turning white at the knuckles from where I had gripped the steering wheel so tightly. I immediately let go and wiped the tears away from my eyes. I fumbled through my glove box trying to find some napkins. In my rush out the door, I failed to bring Kleenex with me. Actually, I didn't forget. I never even thought about Kleenex, but I needed them now. If I couldn't see, I wouldn't be able to drive home. I wiped my eyes and took another deep breath. After looking once more at the letters on the front of the building that read, POLICE STATION, I knew it was presumptuous for me to enter.

I continued to sit there wiping away the tears as I began flipping through the radio stations to find a soothing song. I just needed to regain my composure before driving home. The music might help calm my nerves, and a clear head would be helpful. I passed over some Hispanic stations, and then went to a soft rock one. That did not last long. Within ten seconds I realized that the song was a love song that reminded me of Cal. I flipped back to the previous Hispanic station. I always loved the music, but just never understood the words. My Spanish was mediocre at best. With a large Hispanic population in town, I had learned important words and phrases. The music must have done the trick because I decided that going inside would be the wrong choice. I checked for cars, and then pulled away from the building. We lived close enough that I would be able to stay off the main streets, and avoid additional traffic as I continued to cry.

When I got home, I collapsed once again on the sofa in the living room where Lucy came to my rescue. After crying some more, I decided I needed someone else to wait with me as time passed. I called my best friend, Michelle. We had met about a month after I moved to Albuquerque. She convinced me that I should give biking a try. Now that I think about it, most of our friends came from the bike club. Michelle was an avid cyclist. She competed in road races when she was younger, but turned to mountain bike racing in her mid twenties. She was one of the funniest persons I had ever met. She was always optimistic about everything in life. Michelle was a teacher. She taught eighth grade English and Social Studies. During the summer months, she was a mountain bike tour guide. Albuquerque has a lot of tourism due to its rich history, the hot air balloon industry, and it's perfect climate.

I called Michelle, but she didn't answer her phone either. I decided to leave a text message. If she were up in the mountains for the day, she wouldn't get my message until evening anyway. Who else should I call? What else should I do? I didn't even know. I wasn't the type of person to panic when every little thing didn't go as planned. Yet, in my gut, I could feel that something was wrong. Cal was a very disciplined person. He followed the same routine day after day. I, on the other hand, liked to mix things up. That's why I liked my job so much. It was constantly changing.

Every hour I found myself leaving a text message for Cal. Not once did his phone register that the messages were read. They appeared to be delivered, but not read. I knew that meant that his phone was still in an area that could receive reception. It's hard to get reception in the mountains around here, and once you get passed the park on the west side of the city, reception dies rather quickly. In other words, it seemed likely that he was still in town. There is a lot of dessert in this part of the country with miles of sporadic reception. Maybe I was completely wrong. Maybe he had already traveled outside of the city and was picking up service in another city. My mind continued to wander, sporadically thinking of possibilities. I dismissed every one of them, still in disbelief that I could not reach him.

"Finally," I said when my sister answered the phone.

"Finally what?" she responded back.

"Oh sorry, Rachel," I said. "You just happen to be the first person to answer the phone all day long." It was hard to hear her. "Where are you?" I asked trying to figure out why there was so much noise in the background.

"I'm at the kids swim meet," she said.

"I need to talk to you. Can you go someplace quiet for a few minutes?" I asked knowing that my sister would stop anything to listen.

"Yea, sure, just a second," she said as she walked away from the pool deck. "Carol, can you keep an eye on my kids for a few minutes? I'm talking to my sister," she said faintly into the phone. "Okay, can you hear me now?" she asked.

"Yes, that's better," I said trying to hold back the tears again. "Something really strange happened this morning, Rachel. I'm trying not to panic, but my insides are completely tied in a knot," I told her as I began to explain the events of the day. "I still haven't heard from him. I tried calling his friends and none of them have heard from him. I've been in touch with his office several times, and he still hasn't shown up there either."

"There has to be some type of logical explanation," Rachel said trying to reason that this couldn't be happening.

"Have you called his parents yet?" she asked.

"No. I don't want to alarm them just yet," I responded.

"Did you check the local hospitals?" Rachel asked.

"I checked the med center around the corner from our home, and the urgent care near his work," I told her. "He has not checked into any of those places. He seemed perfectly healthy when he left home."

Rachel tried to be sympathetic. Yet, she felt helpless as well. We both stopped talking for a moment, just pondering the situation before Rachel broke the silence. "I agree with you about the police," she said. "They can't help because not enough time has passed yet. You will probably have to wait until morning, but hopefully he will come home tonight. If I can think of anything else, I'll let you know. In the meantime, I will call you once the swim meet is over."

"Okay. Good bye," I said as we both hung up.

Lucy was whining now as she ran to the back door. In all my confusion, I forgot to let her out. I quickly opened the door before she made a mess over my wide-plank, knotted pine floors. Back inside, she gobbled down her dog food at dinner, while I only picked at my plate. I really wasn't hungry, but had made some Mac-n-Cheese anyway. It was my go-to meal as a kid and all through college. I didn't want to make a huge mess either because I was too tired to clean it up.

I still hadn't heard back from Michelle yet, so I sat in our hammock for a while swinging back and forth listening to the birds and the traffic before taking Lucy on a long walk. She had been waiting all day, and was anxious to go. I don't think I ever missed a day of walking her in the past five years that I owned her. I guess there may have been a day or two when I wasn't feeling well, but on those days Cal walked her.

I reached down and gently placed her black leash and chain collar over her head as her tail wagged uncontrollably. I grabbed two sandwich bags from the pantry along with a brown paper bag, and stuffed them into the pockets of my shorts. I always walked prepared, never giving anyone a chance to accuse me of not properly cleaning up after my dog. Out the door we skirted, barely placing our feet on the last step. We walked through the hillside, and down to the park, past the Old Catholic church perched up on a hill. The sun was just starting to set when we stopped by the church cemetery to rest. We could see the city and all of its neon lights below us. It was a beautiful sight. I just sat there with Lucy looking as far past the horizon into the sun set as I could, hoping and praying this day would somehow turn out differently.

Before long, Lucy and I were back on our feet heading down the hill toward home. We had covered about a two and a half mile loop. My heart was heavy, my muscles ached, and a pounding in my head above my temples caused a weariness that I had not felt in years. Lucy was undoubtedly thirsty as her tongue drooped down towards the rain-deprived terrain. I placed a fresh bowl of water down on the ground as quickly as possible when we arrived home. I then grabbed a clean glass out of the cabinet, filled it with ice, and poured a glass for myself. I drank my water slowly as I watched Lucy gulp hers down. I intentionally left all the lights off when we left the house, hoping I might see one on when we returned. The neighbors' lights were on, but our house stood silently in the dark. There were no signs of Cal anywhere.

I was exhausted when I crawled into bed a short time later. I still had not heard from Michelle, and I could see that Cal had not read my text messages either. Now, if I could only find a way to fall asleep. I was dreary and my eyelids were struggling to stay open. Yet, every time I dosed off a little bit, my mind raced through a maze of possibilities. I needed something to lure me to sleep.

I reached for my computer and double clicked the mouse on Snood. It was a mindless computer game that could induce me into a state of unconsciousness if I played it long enough. That's exactly what I needed tonight, a way to fall asleep. I knew tomorrow would even be worse than today. I just wanted to wake up from this nightmare. In the morning, I would have to call Cal's family.

The four weeks following that Wednesday are somewhat of a blur to me. I remember I slept really well that first night. That's the only night I slept well that I could remember until last night. Every time I crawled into bed, I missed the warm touch of Cal's legs against mine. I missed his muscular arms wrapped around my body. I missed his warmth, and his soft moist kisses. Most of all, I missed the comfort of knowing he was next to me to protect me, and hold me in his arms. I missed everything about him. I missed that we could no longer be together. Last night was the first time in months that I actually slept. I don't know if they drugged me or not, but I slept.

On that first Thursday morning after Cal's disappearance,

I awoke to the sound of music. I wasn't sure where the sound was coming, but in my drowsiness I realized my cell phone was ringing. I had changed my ring tone several months before, but it never occurred to me that it could be my phone. I reached over to the emptiness that occupied my bed that night where I had thrown my cell phone next to Cal's pillow. I had prepared myself that I might be getting that dreadful phone call during the middle of the night. That one phone call that no mother or wife ever wanted to receive. With one eye barely open, I could see that Michelle's number was visible on the screen. She was finally calling back.

Michelle babbled for three or four minutes before I had a chance to say anything other than hello. She told me about her hectic schedule of the previous day, and then she apologized for not calling back earlier. I had completely forgot that yesterday was a school day. All chipper and excited, she finally asked me why I had called the day before. I was still half asleep when I asked her to come over to my house to talk right away. Michelle lived on the east side of the city closer to the mountains, about a fifteen-minute car ride away. I must have fallen back asleep because the next sound I heard was that same music again. It was Michelle a second time. She had been knocking on my front door, but I never heard her. Lucy was on the floor by my bed, and she never budged either.

"Why's the door locked?" Michelle asked when I opened the front door. "And, why are your eyes so red?" she blurted out before realizing that something may be wrong. Michelle knew that we never locked our door ever. I was afraid to leave it unlocked last night. "Did you just get out of bed?" she questioned.

I had fallen asleep in my clothes from the night before. I had changed into shorts and a t-shirt before walking Lucy. I was a morning person, and Michelle knew I hated to sleep in. It was already nine-thirty in the morning, well past my normal wake up. Lucy ran out the front door when I unlocked it. I had completely forgotten about her too.

"Come in," I told Michelle. "Aren't you suppose to be at school right now?" I asked.

"Normally, yes, but not today," she responded gleefully. "The janitor showed up this morning to a water main leak so our building got the day off. Lucky us, I suppose," Michelle explained.

"So, what's up?" Michelle inquired.

That was the beginning of a repeated conversation that took place over and over and over again. Every person I met, and every person who knew Cal or me wanted to hear an explanation. Within an hour, two police officers and detective appeared at my front door step. I don't remember if I called them or if Michelle made the call. It could have been Ann too. She and three employees from Cal's office came over when they didn't hear from me that morning. Then some of our neighbors stopped by when they saw all the traffic coming in and out of our house. It had become Grand Central Station at the Richards residence. I barely recall the conversation I had with my parents or his. My sister flew in from Racine that night. My parents came the following day. Cal's sister, Emma, who lived in Denver showed up at our front door about the same time my parents arrived. Cal's parents, Lincoln and Beverly, only lived about an hour away in Santa Fe. They came immediately upon hearing the news. I don't remember exactly when everyone arrived.

The next several days were spent searching for Cal. His friends called every one of his contacts that I pulled from the records of our phone bill. Some of our cyclist friends took on the responsibility of riding the trails that we rode on a regular basis. There are way too many trails in this part of the country to ride every one. They posted signs at all the trailheads with his photo asking for anyone who sees him to contact the local police.

Cal's employees were amazing. They immediately gathered some hot air balloon enthusiasts and launched an unscheduled flight. That Thursday afternoon they launched twelve balloons that scoured the bike trails that couldn't be reached easily and roof tops of all the buildings downtown. By Friday morning, another twenty-seven balloons were in the air all over town and the outskirts for miles looking for anything that could resemble a body or struggle from an accident. The only thing they found were some abandoned dogs that were left in the desert. They rescued them and brought them back into town to the animal shelter.

The local law enforcement assisted me in filing the necessary paperwork for a missing person. Their focus remained in the vicinity of Cal's warehouse. Unlike me, they were able to access all of the video cameras in the entire region from Planet Fitness to Starbucks, all the way to his office. They confirmed that Joshua and Jason did see Cal standing in front of the 66 Diner just liked Joshua had described to me. To this day, that was his last known location. What Joshua wasn't able to tell me was the event that happened next. Cal started walking towards his office from the diner when three trucks pulled up at a red light at the intersection. At this point, Cal was blocked from all video monitors. The three vehicles included a postal truck, a van from a local flower shop, and a Rio-Cola delivery truck.

According to the police, they questioned and searched the drivers and vehicles from all three of those companies. They did not find any clues or signs of his whereabouts. All three drivers could describe a man on the sidewalk. The florist delivery driver and postal driver even described the clothes that Cal was wearing. They all said that he was carrying a cup in his hands. When all three trucks drove away after the light turned green, Cal was gone. It's possible that he could have walked into the side entrance of the diner, but he wasn't seen on their videotape either. He simply vanished.

It was about three and a half weeks after the incident that I asked the officer in charge if I could see the footage of tape that showed Cal on the scene. First, I wanted to confirm that it was Cal on the video. No one had asked me to confirm earlier if it was even him. Secondly, I wanted to see for myself how someone could disappear so quickly. The officer agreed to show me the tape. I scheduled a time to stop by the police department. I wasn't sure if I would find anything different, but I wanted to see the tape with my own eyes.

"Do you mind if I just sit here awhile and study this film?" I had asked Sergeant Ramirez.

"No, we don't mind at all," he had responded. "Please let Deputy Perez know when you are finished," he had told me. I had been taken to the other side of the police department where an empty cubicle housed a desktop computer. The video had already been pulled up on the monitor for me to view.

"Deputy Perez can escort you back to my office when you are finished," Ramirez had told me. Perez's desk was just around the corner from where I was sitting.

I studied the film over and over again. I must have sat there twenty or thirty minutes trying to find something that the others may not have seen. I couldn't see anything at all out of the ordinary. It looked rather simple. Cal turned the corner, and was walking towards his building located about a half a block away. Trucks pulled up to the light at the corner, then Cal was gone. It happened that quickly. As I sat there, it dawned on me that we had talked about how quickly everything occurred, but no one had ever said how quickly it happened. "How quickly is quickly?" I thought to myself.

I then had a new purpose in viewing the tape. I took my phone out of my handbag, and pulled up the stop clock. The postal truck was the first to pull up to the light. There were no other vehicles in front of it. It had slowed down to a yellow light, and came to a complete stop when the light turned red. It was there for forty-seven seconds before the light turned green. During that time, fourteen cars and three pickup trucks crossed the intersection on the green light. The floral shop van pulled up behind the first truck about five seconds after it came to a stop. Another ten seconds passed before the Rio-Cola trucked pulled up to the stopped traffic in front of it.

If all three drivers had seen Cal, he must have stopped on the sidewalk for at least fifteen seconds. That's how long it took for the Rio-Cola truck to pull up after the light turned red. That driver made a statement identifying Cal as the man he saw. It would not have taken Cal fifteen seconds to walk thirty or forty

35

strides from the corner down pass the van. The video shows Cal passing the van about ten seconds after it came to a stop just as the Rio-Cola truck was pulling up. He must have stopped for a few seconds to drink some coffee, look at his phone, or check his watch. Since we know he passed the van after the van came to a stop, his disappearance happened in the thirty-two seconds that the Rio-Cola truck stopped at the light.

"Exactly how long did each truck stop at the light?" I had asked Sergeant Ramirez when I went back to his office to thank him.

"Oh, I don't really know," he said. "Why?" he then asked.

"I was just wondering," I told him. "Cal's disappearance happened so quickly. I was just thinking that those trucks couldn't have been sitting at the light for too long. Thanks again, Sergeant Ramirez. Please let me know if anything else comes up," I said as I walked away.

I learned more that morning than I ever expected. In the movie industry, attention to detail is extremely important. Timing is everything. The police investigation lacked attention to details. If the Sergeant in charge of the investigation couldn't answer my simple question, then I knew they hadn't invested in this case the way I would. Yes, they confirmed what I had already been told by Joshua. Cal was seen outside the diner. Their investigation stopped though, after their interviews with the truck drivers. Either they didn't ask the right questions or they had already predetermined what the right answers should be to the questions they were asking. Either way, they were content not knowing what happened to Calvin within that half a minute. They had moved on to other more relevant work.

The investigator focused most of his attention on the business. He and his team searched emails and business records trying to find some type of connection with clients or vendors that could have led to a bad contract. As far as I knew, the business was squeaky clean. Never had Cal spoken to me about anything less than an incredible team of employees and highly respectable clients and vendors. I agreed to allow Ryan, the investigator, search thoroughly because I wanted answers. I wanted to know exactly how my husband could vanish so quickly without any evidence of malicious play. His employees all cooperated willingly with the investigator. After a full month searching for clues, he came to the conclusion that some crimes remain mysteries for years. He could not find anything at all wrong with our books, our clients, our employees, or our vendors. He had told me that he would do anything else he could to help with the investigation, but unless some new information was provided it looked like the active investigation would come to an end. I knew there was nothing anyone could do to help. If only someone at the diner had seen what took place outside the window, they would have to come forward and tell the police. Since the diner was closed at that time of day, it was only a handful of workers even there. They were all busy preparing for the day.

My sister was the last relative to vacate my house. She stayed much longer than I ever imagined, a full month away from her kids and family. There wasn't anything more anyone could do for me. I now needed to find a way to get my life back to a new normal, one without Cal. The thought of that made my stomach churn.

Cal's mom called me three or four times a day for the first several weeks after they arrived back home. She did most of the talking- always asking questions and providing suggestions of things I should be doing to help with the investigation. I knew her intentions were virtuous, but I couldn't talk every time she called. Without trying to sound prate, I eventually asked her not to call so often. I promised that I would call her once a week to provide any updates, unless something new emerged. Later, I heard from Emma, that they were glad I put an end to the excessive phone calls. Beverly's anguish and stress tapered a little allowing her some much-needed rest.

Chapter Three
STRIKING HIGH

Christopher was completely understanding of my situation. He gave me four weeks off work. The film that we were starting on that dreaded Wednesday morning was a short film. We decided to let my intern work on my behalf. I had already briefed him on my vision of the set, and how I would accomplish various tasks. The file was sitting on top of my desk available for any staff to embellish. My crew only called me twice in that entire month to ask questions that they couldn't resolve on their own. Christopher called every few days to check on me and to see the status of the investigation. Even though he was my boss, he had become a friend. He wanted me to find Cal as much as I needed to find Cal.

When I began work again, I only worked half days for the next month. I needed to make some adjustments with Striking High. As its new principal, I had to find a way to keep the employees working without Cal at the helm. I wasn't quite ready to give up my job with the movie industry either. Christopher couldn't have been any nicer to me with scheduling. He was a gem.

My situation was completely different than a widow's. There would be no formal venue to express grief, and there would be no closure. A maze of questions continued to exist for everyone. It was easy for my friends to stay informed, but many of Cal's employees and acquaintances did not have direct contact with me after our initial manhunt. It was this group of people that I felt I needed to address on a personal level at his company.

I sent a memo out to the entire staff introducing myself as the new owner prior to our first staff meeting. I wasn't sure what I wanted to do with the business, but I didn't want to make any drastic decisions that I would regret later. I gave everyone the opportunity to speak with me to share their vision of the future of the company. I asked for complete honesty, hoping that any major concerns would be addressed at this time. It also gave them time to express their condolences to me privately. This allowed everyone time to prepare for change. All of his employees had been happy working for Cal, and were hoping to continue at Striking High.

The first thing I learned at Striking High was that we had contracts for the business that would last about eighteen months. I was impressed. I had never talked to Cal about contracts or work budgets. I spent a lot of time listening, watching and asking questions just like I did as a kid when I spent my summers with Rachel at the marina. I learned so much from people way back then. I developed a habit that I still use today… listen first…. ask questions second… don't make any decisions without observing from other points of view.

Cal and I had always agreed with our management style. We believed everyone went through different stages of life that dictated their priorities. For that reason, Cal never had a mandatory scheduled workday. Employees came to work and did their jobs when it was most convenient for them. Cal never had a problem with people not working. Once a month they were required to attend an employee meeting on the first Tuesday of every month. Every employee was given four weeks vacation, but could take more if necessary. Salaries were based on longevity. Cal believed that every job was important, and one position wasn't more important than the next. As a result, his salaries were structured around duration rather than position.

I privately appointed Drew, the Vice President of Operations. He would now have the authority to make decisions necessary with production and operations. Kevin was promoted to Vice President of Finances. Beyond preparing paychecks for everyone, he was now overseeing the entire operational budget for the company. Both Drew and Kevin had been running the show in the interim and were hoping they could continue working jointly together to make the business a success. Both employees were in consensus with this arrangement. We would make it public at the upcoming staff meeting.

Cal's assistant, Ann, would also maintain her role by helping both Kevin and Drew. In addition, she would be working closely with a new employee. Cal had always been involved with the sales and marketing of the company. He actually had a five-year strategic integrated marketing communication plan laid out for the company. This position needed to be filled.

"Thank you," I began when I addressed my new staff for the first time. "I can't begin to thank each and everyone of you enough for your help, support, and encouragement to me during the past several weeks. As you know, this isn't a position I ever expected to be in. Unlike Cal, I plan to take a passive role in the company. Although I am the owner, I want this to be your company. I think Cal has worked hard trying to give you the best support possible so that you can make the best balloons ever. The easiest thing for me to do right now is to lock the doors and not turn back. If I were to do that, not only would my life have been destroyed, but yours also. That's not fair to you or your families. All of you have dedicated many years and long hours in making this company the best in the world. I want to give you the opportunity to continue what you have already successfully done."

I could see smiles and cheers throughout the room as if I had lifted a weight off the employees' shoulders. They were happy. They would all be keeping their jobs.

"After listening to each of you, I have made a few changes that I believe will be beneficial to everyone. First, let me introduce to you our new Vice President of Operations, Drew Hawkings, and our new Vice President of Finances, Kevin Washburn. Drew and Kevin will now be working together to oversee the entire operations of this business. I believe they are the best men capable to lead this company for many years to come. All day-to-day operations will be completely under their control.

The small audience clapped and cheered again when I made the introductions. Ollie, who I had thought was one of the quieter employees, gave a shout out to both men when I made the announcement. "Way to go boys," he said leaning back on his seat.

"In addition, I want to introduce our newest employee,

Jackson O'Reilly. Jackson who is originally from Ireland has spent the past five years in Battle Creek, Michigan, with the Hot Air Balloon Festival organization. He has twenty years experience both here in the United States and Europe with sales and marketing. He will officially begin working next week as the Director of Sales and Marketing. Ann, Drew, and Kevin spent many hours searching and interviewing candidates they believed would be the best fit for this company. I met with the three finalists, and agree that Jackson had the charisma we were hoping to find in our candidate. Please welcome him," I said. Everyone clapped as Jackson raised his hand to acknowledge the introduction.

I had learned from meeting with Drew, Kevin and Ann on several occasions that very few organizational changes were expected to take place. Every employee undeniably loved working at Striking High. They planned to keep the company moving just like Cal had already planned. Internally, the person securing the actual contracts would now be Jackson instead of Cal. Kevin would review the numbers to make sure the contracts were consistent with one another and reflected changes in material costs.

"I have complete confidence in each one of you that Striking High will continue to be robust in the industry, and that you will continue to make it the premier manufacturer of hot air balloons. You may see me come in and out occasionally, but all decisions will be directed through Drew and Kevin. As owner, I will do everything in my power to make this company successful in years to come. This company is for you. I'm sure Calvin would want it this way."

I then turned the meeting over to Drew who expressed his gratitude towards me and wished the circumstances were different. "I never anticipated this role in the company, but I look forward to leading this team," he told the employees. "I will do everything possible to keep this company moving forward." He then proceeded to talk about logistics of the company that related to everyday operations.

For the next four weeks, I met weekly with Drew and Kevin, along with the company's legal advisor. I wanted to make sure that all of the company's legal documents were properly filed. The only hidden news that Cal and I had kept private was the fact that I had always owned fifty percent of the business. He knew there were risks, though minimal, whenever a person entered a hot air balloon. If anything ever happened to him during flight, he wanted to make sure there would be an easy transition with the company so that it could continue to operate flawlessly. Never in a million years did I ever think that I would need to become involved with the business.

The transition ran very smooth. Internally, no one could even tell that there had been a change in management except that Cal's friendly smile never popped in any longer. Our staff continued to deal with the same vendors as they had in the past. The biggest change was for our clients themselves. Cal was no longer the face of Striking High. Jackson was learning his role as the new face of the company. He was dynamic. He was full of life, laughter, and had a charming personality that everyone loved.

I eventually began working full-time again at Albuquerque Studios. The constant change of scenes helped me stay focused on the here and now rather than the past. It had only been three months since my best friend and lover had vanished off the streets of Albuquerque. Coming home at night was the hardest thing for me to do. Lucy tried her best to provide all the love she could, but my four-legged friend couldn't replace the man I loved so much. I was lonely. Our friends tried to get me involved in their activities, and occasionally I would go out to dinner with them. But, it was different now. I couldn't be with them without thinking of Cal. It would never be the same again.

In the last couple of weeks, I have found that I would rather spend time with Michelle or my friend from work, Felicia. She began working at the studios about seven years ago, but our friendship really developed about four years ago. Several months after her husband passed away from cancer, I asked her if she wanted to spend the day with me because her boys were spending the weekend with their grandparents. I felt bad for her and didn't think she would want to stay home alone all weekend. I vividly remember asking her if she would like to go on a short ride with me on a Saturday morning before the heat of the sun got too intense. I thought she would decline the invite. "I would love to go with you," she claimed. I was very surprised that she accepted the invitation.

After our ten-mile ride through one of the local parks in town, we briefly parted our ways to clean up prior to lunch. We then went to a local art festival where I picked out a few pieces that I thought I could use for an upcoming set. A bronze sculpture of a stallion was the steal of my day. I would have paid several hundred dollars more, if they had priced it higher. We finished the day with dinner and a movie. Cal was out of town on business that weekend, so it worked out perfectly. Felicia is eight or nine years older than me, but loves the same things that I love. I never knew that my simple act of kindness would lead to a lasting friendship.

Chapter Four
A LITTLE PIECE OF PARADISE

"Rachel," I said one day. "I can't do this. I realize only a few shorts months have passed, but I can't continue to come home to our empty house. I cry myself to sleep almost every night, only to wake during the night thinking of Cal and the days we shared together. I get up every morning, put a fake smile on my face, and hope to prove to everyone around me that I am a strong woman when I arrive to work. I'm only kidding myself," I explained. "This isn't normal. Someone can't disappear that easily," I continued.

"You're right," Rachel responded. "I don't get it either. You need to give yourself some time. I know time doesn't heal every wound, but it helps. Maybe you should move. Sell your house and move out to North Valley. You and Cal always talked about moving out there someday when you have a family. Maybe someday should be now," she said. "Consider all the benefits - a new beginning for you, peace and quiet away from city traffic, and a large yard for Lucy to run around. You might even be able to find a place that needs a little work. A new project could be therapeutic for you. Plus, you would be a lot closer to many of the bike trails that you ride on a regular basis," she added.

"What if Cal reappears out of nowhere and comes

home?" I asked.

"Caroline, I know it's only been a short time, but you have to move on with your life. Maybe you will meet one of those wealthy young men who live out that way," she said.

"But, I don't want to meet anyone," I said. "I just want my old life back with Cal."

Rachel paused for a moment. "Sis," she said, "I know you love Cal and I know Cal loved you. If Cal does reappear, he's smart enough to find you. He discovered you once. He can discover you again. He knows your number."

Then I asked the question that none of us have spoken about, even in the hours immediately following his disappearance. The question that has crossed by mind countless times before, and one that others probably have discussed behind my back. "Rachel," I said, "do you think Cal left me on his own? Do you think he left me for another woman?"

Without any hesitation at all, she immediately responded, "No way. He didn't look like a man trying to run or hide from you. There were no signs of any wrong doing at all. His computer was clean. His business was growing and operating efficiently according to both staff and the detective. There have been no signs of another girl or anything else. I don't know what happened to him. Maybe there was a car waiting for him in his own parking lot. We will never know. If something fishy had been going on, I think it would have leaked out by now."

"I agree. I just needed to hear that from someone other than me," I told her. "I think it's kind of strange that no one has ever mentioned this before, but it has crossed by mind many times."

"Doug and I talked about it, but decided there was absolutely no evidence to back up that theory," Rachel continued. "If he were having an affair, something would have shown up with the investigation. There wasn't even a single phone call that could not be identified. No money was missing from your account. No credit cards were used, and his cell phone has remained untouched since that dreadful day."

I couldn't fathom that possibility. "We were getting along great. Never once did he act strange, differently, or even try to hide anything from me," I told my sister. "I'll give your suggestion some thought- maybe a move would be the best thing for me. Give the kids a big hug from their favorite aunt too."

"Oh, I will," she said. "I'll talk to you later. Goodbye."

Rachel was right. I needed to make a drastic change beyond the one that already took place. This change would be for me, one that I approved. The only way for me to stop mourning Cal was to change my environment at home. There isn't a day that goes by that I don't think about him a thousand times. I miss him so much. I don't know if he's safe, dead, or alive. Maybe he's wishing he were back home too. I just don't know. With every day that goes by, my chances of ever seeing him again diminish. And, if by the grace of God that I do see him again, he probably would be happy that I actually made the move. He would want me to be happy and try to find happiness again.

For the next several hours, I pondered the question that Rachel raised. I couldn't get it out of my mind. Later that evening when I took Lucy on her daily walk, my heart felt different as I walked through our neighborhood. In days past, I always strived to be a part of our little niche. I attended all the block parties, spoke with everyone when I walked Lucy, and I even bought lemonade from all the kids who set up their little stands. I knew everyone within four blocks of our home.

Today when I walked, I felt disconnected from the neighbors for the first time ever. The bond that Cal and I always felt to our community was gone. I almost felt like a stranger walking down a street in a far away city. The five-year-old twins who live on the next block always pet Lucy when they are playing outside. Today they were drawing with chalk on their front sidewalk. When I commented that I liked their artwork, they barely said "hello" to me. They didn't even acknowledge the dog.

Then it occurred to me that the entire neighborhood seemed distant. The first few weeks after Cal's disappearance, everyone went out of his or her way to see me. Now they seem to go out of their way to avoid me. Maybe people are afraid to talk to me anymore because they don't know what to say. Just last week, when Marilyn Whitley was pulling weeds from her flowerbed near the sidewalk, she turned and walked to her back yard when I was only a few houses away. Jack Meadows, who makes his living as a courier, usually leaves a treat for Lucy on the step of his front porch. We haven't seen one there in several weeks. And, no one has invited me over for hamburgers or brats in a while. Cal and I used to go to the Wixoms or Charleys every few months, but neither of them has even called since hearing about Cal. Maybe everyone is busy or they are simply afraid to hurt my feelings by saying the wrong thing. Regardless, they have made the situation worse by ignoring me.

"Lucy," I said, "I think it's time for you and me to find

a new home." She looked at me with her piercing brown eyes and wagged her tail.

The very next day, I left a message for our realtor. "Hi Robert. It's me, Caroline," I said. "I think I would like to sell our home and move to North Valley. Can you help me?" I asked. "Please call me back. Thanks."

Robert helped Cal and me find our current home. We tried finding one on our own, but at the time we bought this house, the market was slim. There were very few homes for sale, and the ones that were on the market had sold for full asking price or more. The market was better now, and I was hopeful that I could find something reasonable. Cal and I always wanted a large home with a large yard and pool. As much as we loved to bike, it sure would be nice to come home to a refreshing pool. I wanted a yard with green grass. It sounds like a simple request, but in this part of the country grass is a commodity.

I leaned up from my bent over position on my hands and knees to peer out the window to look at the two Arabian fillies across the street. A smile crossed by face for the first time in months. I could see the progress of my project, and the beauty of those young horses. They were intriguing to watch, and their muscles were so defined even at this young age. "Breathtaking." That is the word I mumbled to myself out loud as they caught my eye. I had only been in the house a few short weeks, but was spellbound on numerous occasions by their presence.

My favorite one was a solid dark chocolate colored

horse with a single mark between her fore head of a diamond that trailed slightly down her nose between her eyes. She stood slightly taller than her companion, but could prance gingerly with her outstretched neck across the field. I don't know her name. Matter of fact, I didn't even know that she was a girl until four days ago when I met the neighbor for the first time. As I was retrieving my mail at the end of my driveway, Martin pulled up in his white four-door pickup truck to welcome me to the neighborhood. I believe he said that his last name is Ka'trera, but I don't know for sure. I told him how I loved watching his horses. He shared with me that the two in the field directly across from my house were his two-year-old fillies. He invited me to stop over anytime to meet his family, and to see the rest of his horses. I told him I would come once I settled in and finished some of my projects around the house.

The second horse was chestnut in color and had very skinny, long legs. She reminded me of a baby doe whose body was not proportioned with her legs yet. Her entire body was solid in color like the other one except the bottom fourth of her legs were completely white. A white line drizzled down her nose and faded into the black tip of her snout. Her mane was a darker brown with white tips like her legs. She too was beautiful, but not as graceful as her counterpart.

It never occurred to me to ask Martin the horses' names, so I decided to nickname them only yesterday. Lady Hershey was the semisweet chocolate colored horse that I named after my favorite candy bar. We didn't go on many vacations as a kid, but I will always remember our trip to Philadelphia when we stopped at the Hershey factory for a tour on our way home. I nicknamed the other one, Sweet Chestnut. Her color reminded me of the chestnuts my grandmother used to roast over an open fire each Christmas Eve when we visited. I can almost smell them now, just thinking about their enticing aroma.

After receiving a dose of inspiration from the view, I began working again. My last four weekends and evenings had been engulfed in a sea of paint and stain as I refreshed the walls and added life to the floors. New flooring in the entrance would add a welcoming dimension that this house needed. I wanted a lighter floor with large rectangular shaped tile that would be inviting and welcoming. I liked the coolness of ceramic tile down here, but it was uncomfortable to stand on for any length of time.

I finished applying a thin layer of adhesive to the sub floor as I prepared to lay twelve by twenty-four inch tiles in my entry. My hands were sticky from touching the edges of the tiles against the floor as I laid them in off setting rows. The tile was a newer product that was much thicker than normal vinyl tile. It actually resembled ceramic tile, but was softer to the touch. It would hold up against the scurry and shuffle of Lucy's paws running across the floor.

The old rolled vinyl flooring, which was now piled in broken pieces in a garbage can, needed replaced. It was the eyesore of this property. The ceramic-looking tile resembled a tone white marble with gray veins. The gray was a near match to the new tile I had already installed in the kitchen. I had removed the flooring in the entry two days earlier. Hidden beneath the carpet throughout the main floor were beautiful wood floors. A few stains on the floor must have prompted previous owners to carpet.

I had found the perfect home in North Valley that I could remodel on my own to make it more comfortable. A few minor cosmetic changes were all this house needed. It had a new kitchen and remodeled master bath. I brightened the walls with vibrant colors that reflected the culture of Albuquerque. The previous owners were elderly and had lived with the ugliest mauve imaginable. Robert told me that the couple's son had demanded they replace the kitchen and bath cabinetry prior to selling the home. Apparently, they listened to him because both were remarkably nice. The flooring needed work.

"This is the perfect house for you," Felicia had said as we stepped inside the third house that Robert showed us on a Saturday morning just eight weeks ago. We had not even walked in the house yet, and she knew it was the one for me. She was not at all concerned about the interior of the home. She had worked closely with me for years now, designing and overseeing the production of sets for the studio. She knew I could liven up any place.

"Felicia," I said, "How do you even know? We haven't walked through it yet."

"I just have a good feeling," she said. "How could you go wrong with a horse farm across the street?" she had asked.

She was right. This was the perfect house. It was a four bedroom contemporary ranch that sat on an acre of land. The pulchritude out front enhanced the walkout in the back. I felt I was walking into paradise every time I stepped foot outside.

A large stone fireplace with built-in gridiron would provide the perfect accommodations for grilling outdoors. A bright

orange, cobalt and slate countertop yielded five feet of countertop on both sides of the fireplace. Three sets of fifty-four inch
round glass top tables with four rod iron chairs were nestled off
to the side. Large orange umbrellas hovered over each table.
The cushion covers for each chair needed reupholstered, but
that was no big deal. I'm sure one of our seamstresses at work
would be willing to help me with that detail. The outdoor furniture came with the house.

"Oh my word," Felicia gasped when we walked out back
for the first time. "Is this a vineyard cafe?" she asked.

"This is exactly what I need," I responded back. "Not
only is it beautiful, but it's also enchanting."

The main attraction beyond the spectacular grill was the
pool and waterfall. No wonder the previous homeowners didn't
spend more money on the inside of their home. They had made
the outside perfect. It was a little piece of paradise with the
mountains in the background.

The pool was rather large with a walk-in shallow end
that gradually dropped to nine feet. A spectacular waterfall that
featured a diving platform above stood high above the pool at
the far end. Coming through the center of the waterfall was a
slide that we didn't even notice on our first trip to the house.

At that moment in time, I knew without a shadow of
doubt that I wanted to buy this house. Felicia and I had only
seen the entry, living room and kitchen, but I didn't care if the
house had some hidden quirky features. I could totally live
here. And, if by some miracle, Cal returned, he would love this
place.

"Robert," I said, "Please cancel the showings for the remaining homes we are suppose to see today."

"Are you sure, Caroline?" he asked me.

"Yes, we're sure," Felicia piped in. "Can you put an offer in right now?" she asked.

"Sure, I guess we can do that," Robert said. "Let me go out to my car to get the paperwork," he added.

Felicia and I then walked through the remainder of the house on our own while Robert prepared to write an offer. The master bedroom was grand. It also featured French doors that opened onto the back terrace and pool. The three bedrooms were along the front side of the house, the street side. Their views were amazing too. The horse farm across the street was spectacular. Everyday fifteen or sixteen horses grazed in the fields. It was the fillies that I adored.

"Robert," I said when we reentered the dining area where he was sitting at the table. "Do you think I might be able to come back tonight? I want Michelle to see this place too."

"Well, if my wife doesn't mind, I think it will be fine. The owners are out of town for the weekend," he said.

"Maybe you could bring her along with you. I'm sure she would love to see this place," I said. "Afterwards, we could go for dinner at Sandiago's. My treat," I added. "Felicia, you are welcome to join us too."

"Thanks, but I have plans to take the kids horse back riding this afternoon and out for dinner. I'm sure they won't want to trek back out here with me," she said.

"Do you have a number in mind?" Robert asked, not sure if he should ask with Felicia present.

"Let's go with five thousand one hundred and eleven

dollars over asking price," I said without hesitation. I'm sure they will be receiving other bids as well, and I don't want to lose this place.

Later that evening Robert and his wife, Roxanne, met Michelle and me at the house. Michelle loved the place. The pool was incredible at night. The waterfall was featured with spectacular outdoor lights changing colors to the rhythm of music being played through hidden loud speakers. Robert had learned later that afternoon from the listing realtor how to turn on the lights and music. He came a few minutes early to open the house and turn on the lights for us. It was spectacular.

Four weeks later, I was given the keys to my new house, a place I was hoping would become my home. I had returned a third time when the inspections were made to measure the flooring because I wanted to order supplies in advance for any remodeling that I wanted to do. Basically, it came down to flooring and paint. I would eventually change some of the light fixtures, but I would wait until I lived there a while to see what I really wanted to change.

I had set a deadline for myself. I wanted to get the few cosmetic things done right away before I unpacked. That would eliminate the need to move things out of the way a second time. I took possession of the house one week before I moved my furniture from my house. I would have preferred to paint and then refinish the wood floors, but I needed to get the floors done first before moving the furniture in. I would need help moving the larger pieces so this would work out better for me. The deliverymen could place all the furniture in the center of each room away from the walls until I was done painting. My friends would help me with the pieces I couldn't handle on my own.

I grabbed my tape measure and pencil to mark the piece that needed cut. The blade to my knife wasn't as sharp as it had been when I started, but I only had a few cuts remaining that needed to go under the base board. I was almost done. I finished laying the other full pieces of tile.

"Yes," I thought. I am finished. I stood up and stretched my legs. "Lucy," I said as she tried to jump over my barricade of dining chairs. "I'm done. You can run all over the house wherever you want to go, tomorrow. How's that girl?" I then stepped over the chair as Lucy rubbed against my legs.

With clean hands and my tools stashed away in the garage, Lucy and I went out back for a glass of ice, cold lemonade and a game of fetch. Lucy loved her new yard, and life without a leash. She could roam freely.

Chapter Five
MINUTE DETAIL

Every few days I retreated to the video that I copied onto my cell phone from the footage I received at the police station of Cal's last day. All of my family and close friends know that I went down to the police station to watch it, but I never told anyone that I actually copied it for myself.

It had been four weeks since I last spoke with anyone from the police station, only to hear that no new leads had been received. Basically, it was their way of saying, that no one is actively investigating his disappearance anymore.

I had the video memorized by now, but still hoped that some new piece of evidence would jump out at me if I continued to watch it. After the invasion of friends and relatives and the minimal restructuring of Cal's business, I began a new routine every morning on the way to my office. I would drive by the neighborhood that Cal used to walk to work. Once a week I would stop by the coffee shop to buy a muffin. I am not a coffee drinker so stopping there daily seems pointless to me. On some days, I would go to the diner for breakfast. Other days, I simply would walk up and down the street for fifteen minutes just absorbing the details that I had never noticed before.

I didn't know if I was looking for something specifically, but I thought I would familiarize myself with the neighborhood.

Maybe in time, I would find something extraordinary that would help me piece together his disappearance. I knew my chances were slim, but I made a three-month commitment to myself to stick with this plan.

At first I didn't notice anything unusual, but then I noticed something different a few weeks into my three-month plan. The Rio-Cola truck seemed to drive by nearly the same time every day at 7:59 am. I decided to park across the street to observe. I saw the postal truck three times around that same time, and I have only seen the floral delivery truck once. The thing that struck me about the Rio-Cola truck is that it came by here consistently every single day at 7:59 am. On the morning that Cal disappeared, it came by at 7:53 am. It was six minutes earlier than normal on that dreaded Wednesday. I realize it's hard to be that accurate, but there was another thing different about the truck. The driver has been the same person every single day too, but he was not the driver in Cal's video.

I can understand if there are different drivers periodically, but Sergeant Ramirez had told me that the driver had been on this same route for three years now. Although they both look similar, this clearly was not the same driver. The day my husband disappeared, a different truck and driver drove this route.

For the past twenty-one days, I have relocated my observation point to observe the intersection at the corner of the diner. If Sergeant Ramirez ever viewed any more tape, he would see that I have been here every day for weeks. Not once has he called me to follow-up. I called and spoke to his assistant four weeks ago, but decided that would be my last call to him. He never calls me and seems disinterested in the case now. Since there is no evidence of homicide, I don't think he was ever interested in the case.

Every day I have been documenting the exact time and driver of the truck as it drives past the diner. After three weeks of observation, I noticed something new today for the first time ever. It was clear to me why I had not noticed anything different about the truck before. I had not been close enough to the truck to see specific details.

Yesterday, I parked my truck two blocks away and timed my appearance perfectly. I wanted to walk to the diner just as the Rio-Cola truck would be driving by. Today, the driver pulled up to the traffic light just as the truck had done every morning. It wasn't the same truck as in the video. The video shows a very small Mexican flag in the lower left corner of the truck, just above the bumper with the identification number of 053171 in white block letters. This truck has the identical numbers of 053171, but no flag.

My mind immediately went into a frenzy again. "Why Rio-Cola?" I thought to myself. "There must be some type of connection. Was Cal in the midst of a deal with Rio-Cola?" I wondered. Unlike most people in this region, Cal and I didn't even like Rio-Cola. We preferred other soft drinks.

It was difficult staying focused at work. I was glad it was a Friday because I needed the weekend to collect my thoughts on this new piece of evidence. My mind clearly was in a different place, and back on Cal again. I rushed home to find Lucy patiently waiting for me. She had become my best friend all over again. She loved her new space, and was always excited for me to come home each night.

I placed a filet mignon on the grill with a skillet of sautéed mushrooms, yellow and orange peppers, and sweet onions. I then placed a cup of water into a pan to boil for instant rice. All my meals had become rather simple once Cal disappeared. With this wonderful outdoor grill, I spent most of my time grilling rather than cooking anymore. It was simple and easy, and convenient when preparing a meal for only myself.

After pouring a glass of cabernet sauvignon, I walked back outside to refresh Lucy's water bowl. The routine was becoming more and more familiar to Lucy. We played fetch almost every day while I was grilling. It was the same routine last night. I refreshed her bowl, turned the steak over, stirred the vegetables, and grabbed her tennis ball. Back and forth she ran retrieving the now slobber-stained ball. She loved the game, and loved the attention she was receiving all to herself. The best part was the treat she would receive when the game was over. Cal and I used to feed her just regular dry dog food. Now, I decided I would treat her with my leftovers. She knew if the grill was on that she was bound to have some type of meat.

This morning when I woke up, I had planned to go for a short ride after dinner. I love to take my bike out on Friday nights for a short ride. It helps me relax from a long week at work. My plans changed after my morning discovery. Instead, I would sit by the pool with my computer to research. I might even swim a few laps later. I wanted to dig through our computer files at Striking High. I had secured access to all our accounts when I took over the business, but I had never used them before. I never felt the need to get on line when I met periodically with Drew, Kevin, and Ann. They always kept me informed with important news. No one spoke about Cal anymore. I think they were afraid to mention his name in front of me.

I searched our client database, and future clients, but came up short. I then checked our financial software to see which vendors might be connected to Rio-Cola. The only name that appeared was Albuquerque Bottling Company. That was the company that provided beverages for our vending machine. We had catered a number of events in recent years and those names appeared as well. Other than that, I could not find anything that would have a connection with beverages at all.

I did learn one thing. There is a difference between American Rio-Cola and Mexican Rio-Cola. According to the Internet, Mexican Rio-Cola is smoother and better tasting. It uses cane sugar as a sweetener, unlike the American prototype that uses high fructose corn syrup. The Mexicans in this area, which make up a large percentage of population on the south side of town, will only drink Mexican Rio-Cola.

I would have to ask Felicia about this. I've seen her drink Rio-Cola many times, but never heard anything about one kind tasting better than the next.

I slipped out of my loosely hanging peach cover up, and walked into the pool with Lucy at my side. I loved the feeling of the warm water as it crept up my almost barren body. When I reached the deep end, I dove into the water to fully emerge my head. It was refreshing. When I came up for a breath of air, the water rolled down over my face filling my empty mouth that was cracked just enough to wet my tongue. I felt new all over again. Lucy splashed around in the shallow end waiting for me to return.

I guess I never realized how much I missed the water until now. I was experiencing a little piece of paradise every day in my own back yard. I'm sure glad that Cal had moved in with me when we got married, rather than me moving in with him. I wouldn't have been able to sell the house, if it had been the other way around.

I sat in the shallow end playing with Lucy for a while when my phone rang. I grabbed a towel hanging on the hook before reaching for the phone. It was Michelle.

"Are you ready for the party on Sunday?" she asked when I answered.

"Well, I think so," I told her. "I already bought the burgers and dogs. Everyone else is planning to bring a dish or chips. I might need to buy some beer for the guys," I told her. I didn't drink beer so I never kept any in the house. There was no better time to have a house warming party than for the Super Bowl.

"You're going to love my new recipe for guacamole," Michelle told me.

I completely disregarded her statement. Food was the last thing I wanted to talk about right now. "Hey, would you like to go on an errand with me in the morning?" I asked her. Saturday couldn't come too soon. I wanted to investigate the Rio-Cola bottling company and the bottling company that services Striking High.

"Sure," Michelle said.

"Meet me here at six then," I told her before hanging up.

"Six?" she said. "Why so early?" It's a Saturday," she complained. "Is everything okay?"

"You'll see tomorrow," I told her.

Chapter Six
COWBOY BOOTS

I didn't sleep well last night, so morning came rather early. Instead of taking a long, hot shower, I decided to shock myself awake. There was no better way of waking up than jumping into the pool. I quickly undressed and flew open the door with Lucy trailing behind me. I ran straight for the deep end, and made a cannon ball splash. I think my heart skipped a beat as I sunk to the bottom of the pool. It was an invigorating feeling though. My lungs closed heavy on my chest as I held my breath long enough to push off from the bottom of the pool with both feet to rocket myself back to the top. I felt energized.

The water was cooler than I expected, and the adrenaline certainly woke me up. I swam to the shallow end almost as fast as I had run into the pool. I was definitely awake now, and ready to start my day's journey. "I sure hope no one was spying on me this early in the morning," I thought as I raced for my towel. I didn't wear a suit. As I pondered that thought for a brief moment, it dawned on me that it would be impossible to spy around here without a telescopic lens.

I raced back into my room where I got dressed and quickly brushed my teeth. I had learned about the two-minute rule when I was young, but I think I broke that record this morning with a twelve-second count. I simply did not care. I consistently brushed my teeth two or three times a day, so breaking the rule this morning was meaningless. In the time it took me to brush my teeth, Lucy had used her dog run and was running back through the open door when I walked out of the bathroom. I locked the door behind her and race-walked down the hallway, passed the living room into the kitchen where I grabbed some dog treats and water for Lucy, and an orange juice and muffins for Michelle and me.

"Get in," I told Lucy as she jumped into the back of the truck, her tail wagging so fast that her head was spinning. She loved the days when she could tag alongside me with her head hanging out of the back seat window. She especially loved the wind blowing on her face. She was the perfect travel companion, never complaining about the type of music being played or how often we stopped. She was always ready for an adventure.

Michelle was pulling into the driveway, just as I was pulling the Land Rover out of the garage. My lease was about to expire, but I had not given any thought at all to what type of vehicle I would get next. I should probably add that task to my to-do-list.

"Wow, you're in a hurry," Michelle said as she got into the front seat after parking her car in the turn around.

"Well, I have places to be right now," I told her, as I looked both ways before backing out of my driveway. "I'll fill you in on the details as we go." I was definitely on a mission this morning.

"So, what's going on?" Michelle asked. "You're a little too wired for this to be about the big game tomorrow," she said.

Michelle and I had planned my "housewarming" party

for tomorrow when my friends could see the house and enjoy the Super Bowl game at the same time. I had completed the flooring and painting, changed out some hardware on the bathroom cabinets, unpacked most of my boxes, and had moved my furniture into place. I still wanted a new lamp for my bedroom and a chandelier for the dining room, but those items would come later when I found something that I really liked. I had been so busy fixing the place up that I had not done any shopping for new items yet, and I had no plans to buy on-line until I shopped locally first.

"I think I found something," I told Michelle.

"What do you mean?" she then asked as the tone of her voice changed to one more serious.

"I think I found a clue about Cal's disappearance," I began to explain. I told her about the picture I had of the three trucks, and how the Rio-Cola truck seemed to be different than the one that drove that route daily. "I just want to check it out."

"Is that where we are going now?" Michelle asked. "To the Rio-Cola plant?"

"Yep," I said. "It's Saturday morning, the day before the Super Bowl. Either all those trucks have additional routes today, or they all should be parked. I want to see what's happening with them, and to see if I can find the one truck that was in the video."

It took us nearly twenty-five minutes to drive to the other side of town where the bottling company was located. I had googled directions the night before, so I knew exactly where I was headed. I had my camera with me along with binoculars. We decided to park about a block from the building on a side street under a tree. The shadow of the tree would hide our faces, yet we would be close enough to see whether any trucks entered and left the facility.

I handed Michelle the old binoculars that belonged to my grandpa. They were still in their original brown leather case with carrying strap. The leather was cracked and worn, and the strap was broken. When I unpacked my boxes a week ago and rediscovered my lost treasure, I knotted the broken strap and put the binoculars in my middle console. I knew they would come in handy at some point. I just didn't think it would be this soon. The binoculars appeared brand new at first glance. It didn't take Michelle but two seconds to comment how good the zoom was with the binoculars. "Yea, isn't it?" I commented back. "Those used to belong to my grandpa. Nobody in the family wanted them when he passed away, so I took them. I thought I would use them for bird watching or something like that- not this." Michelle and I both chuckled.

I then reached behind the passenger seat to grab my camera bag. I had three lenses for my camera - the zoom, macro, and telescopic. Today, I wanted to use the telescopic lens since we were several hundred yards away from the plant entrance. I exchanged lenses, and finally settled down long enough to take a deep breath. I began nibbling at my muffin as we waited. Michelle had eaten her muffin within minutes of leaving my house and Lucy had gobbled up several treats as well.

It was sleepy for the first twenty minutes with very little traffic entering or exiting the parking lot. Two roadrunners in the barren field next to the parking lot caught Michelle's attention. At first glance, they appeared to be dancing in the open lot. After observing them for several minutes, Michelle came to the conclusion that they were leaping into the air to catch insects. Nonetheless, they provided entertainment that we did not expect to see. They even caught Lucy's attention. I'm sure she would have chased after them like a rabbit or squirrel, if I had let her out of the truck. I diverted her attention by giving her some more treats and water.

Michelle was the first to see a row of trucks pull around from the back corner of the building, headed towards the street. One by one, they turned different directions going on their respected routes. Not a single truck had a flag sticker on it. Michelle could see the disappointment on my face when the last truck drove by without the matching number. As we discussed what our next stop should be, three more trucks pulled around from the far side of the building. One truck was heading our way. It was the 053171 truck.

"Let's follow him," I told Michelle as he pulled out onto the main street. After he passed, two other cars passed us before we could pull out onto the main street as well. That would be perfect. He would never pay attention to us anyway.

"At least, he's easy to see," Michelle laughed. "Is it the same driver?" she asked curiously.

"I'm not sure," I replied. "Let's first see where he goes," I added. "I'll be able to tell when he gets out for his delivery whether he's the right man or not."

About five miles away, the truck pulled into the side lot of a convenient store. We pulled into a Texaco station across the street. If it was the same driver, I didn't want him to see my face. If he had been interviewed as the police chief had said, then he probably knew who I was already.

The first thing we saw as the driver stepped down out of his cab was his cowboy boots. "Isn't that odd?" I commented to Michelle. We still couldn't see the cowboy's face. His back was turned towards the truck as he stepped down. He was tall, and had light brown hair combed back over his ears. It was all one length and fell onto his shoulders.

"What's odd, Caroline?" Michelle asked in return.

"The cowboy boots… I think it's very peculiar that a delivery man would be wearing cowboy boots for work," I explained.

"Yea, but people wear cowboy boots all the time around here," she defended.

"When was the last time you saw a delivery truck driver wearing cowboy boots to work?" I then asked.

Michelle paused a moment. "I don't know," she finally said. "The real question is whether he's the right guy or not?" she asked.

His back had been turned to us so we couldn't see his face initially. After looking down at his clipboard, he walked a few paces towards the middle of the truck where he opened a compartment. It was full of cola. He placed ten cartons onto a two-wheel cart, and then turned towards the entrance. I grabbed my camera and snapped a few shots hoping to get one of his face. As he walked inside, he turned slightly, long enough for me to snap a side view shot. I zoomed in and could see that this was the driver who had been driving the route for the last several weeks. This was, according to Sergeant Ramirez, the regular driver of this route. He looked very similar to the other driver, but I wasn't a hundred percent sure if he was the same man in the picture.

It was only seventeen minutes after seven. I then explained to Michelle that he was very precise in the time he traveled through the intersection by Diner 66. "He must have at least one more stop between here and there," I commented.

He was inside for two more minutes before returning to his truck. I snapped a few more pictures of him as he strapped the two-wheeler onto a cart rack on the back of the truck with a bungee cord and climbed back into the cab. He sat in the cab another two minutes before pulling out onto the street again.

"You would think he would want to quickly finish his route since it's a Saturday," Michelle imagined. "I sure would if this were my route."

"Yea, me too," I agreed.

We waited for several cars and pickup trucks to pull out in front of us before we entered the street. We didn't want him to notice that we were following him. He was quite a ways down the road in front of us now. He drove another two miles before pulling into another parking lot. This stop was to the back of a local grocery store.

"Let's pull ahead of him, Caroline," Michelle recommended. "You already know where he's heading next. Then we won't look suspicious at all."

"I have a better idea Michelle. Let's go to this grocery store. You can go inside and buy beer. Maybe you can get a real up close look of him since he'll be in the same isle as you," I suggested.

"What am I looking for?" Michelle asked hesitantly.

"I don't know… maybe tattoos, a fancy watch, or anything else that might lead to more clues," I said.

"Well, okay. I'll give it a try," she agreed as she opened the door. "What kind of beer do you want?" she asked.

"I don't care. Whatever you think the guys will like the most," I said as she hurried across the parking lot into the store.

While Michelle was inside, I scrambled through the video on my phone to get the best still shot of the driver. I then compared my new shots with the ones I had already taken when I made my discovery. I couldn't tell for sure if all the drivers were the same. I was rather confident that this driver was the same as the man who has been driving ever since the dreadful day. I wasn't sure if he was the same man in the video.

Six minutes later Michelle was back in the parking lot carrying a twelve pack of Miller Light and a smile on her face. I knew something had happened in there just the way she gloated and pranced back to the Land Rover.

"What did you do now?" I asked Michelle when she opened the back door to put the beer on the floorboard out of Lucy's way. "I know something's up because of that crazy smirk that you can't wipe off your face."

"His name is Philip," she said as she bounced into the front seat. "And, his phone number is 505.232," she began to say before I interrupted her.

"You have his phone number too?" I blurted out. "His name and his phone number?"

"Yep. And, better yet, I'm going out with him tonight," she said. "He's got the sexiest voice, Caroline. I couldn't resist. I need to meet him downtown at 7:00 pm at Tucanos."

"But, Michelle," I protested. "He could be dangerous."

By now, Philip had pulled the truck around and was back on the main street. Again, we followed behind multiple cars so he couldn't see that we were tracking him.

"You honestly think a man who has been driving the same route for the past three years is dangerous," she asked.

"Well, something isn't right. How on earth can he time his appearance at that intersection so perfectly each and every day? Do you realize how many red lights there are from here to there, let alone the traffic?" I asked. "That's beside the point. How did you get a date so dang quickly?"

"It was the cowboy boots," Michelle responded.

"What?" I asked.

"It was the cowboy boots. I timed it just perfectly. All the colas were lined up on one side of the isle and the beers on the other. Miller products were exactly across the isle from the Rio-Cola products. As he bent down to stack a carton onto the next one, I bent over slightly so he would bump into me. Sure enough he did. He quickly apologized and after that I said, 'Damn, I like your boots.' He responded, 'Really?' Then I said, "Yea, I've never seen a delivery man wearing cowboy boots to work before." Next thing I know he asked if I wanted to go out on a date."

"Did he come up with Tucanos, or you?" I asked.

"Well, he asked what sounded good to me, and Tucanos was the first thing that came to mind. I just blurted it out. We then exchanged names and numbers. It was that simple," Michelle explained.

"You actually gave him your name and phone number?"

I questioned.

"Well, I fibbed a little," she continued. "I gave him my middle name. I told him I was Quinn. If he's an innocent man, and we start dating, then I can work my first name back into the picture without much hassle."

"You actually like this guy?" I asked knowing that Michelle was acting rather giddy.

"He's hot, Caroline. Who wouldn't be interested in him?" she responded back.

"Did you actually give him your real phone number?" I questioned.

"I gave him the cell number that I use for school. You know how each year I buy a cheap phone with prepaid minutes that I pass out to my students and their parents?" she asked.

"Yes," I said.

"Well, rarely does anyone ever call me on that phone. Most correspondence is done through e-mail instead. I always end the school year with additional minutes. I gave him that number, so if things don't work out he'll only have my number for a couple more months. I'll burn through the extra minutes at the end of the year, pitch it, and get a new phone at the start of next school year," she explained.

"I'm glad you didn't give him your real cell number, I said as we approached the diner.

"Quick, Caroline, pull over," Michelle said as she pointed towards the Rio-Cola truck.

The truck had stopped on the side of the road and turned on its hazard lights. Philip did not get out. He had pulled up in front of a small neighborhood park that was two blocks from

Cal's warehouse. Caroline looked at her watch. Philip was five minutes earlier than normal. The diner was just three blocks down the road.

"Why would he need to wait?" I asked in disbelief. I couldn't believe that he actually had stopped. We anxiously waited the five minutes to see what would happen next. As quickly as the truck had come to a halt, it started up again passing the diner precisely at 7:59 am.

"Maybe he stops to make a phone call each morning," Michelle said trying to convince herself that her date would be fine.

"Let's keep following him," I said. I just think it's a strange coincidence that he comes through here at the exact time each day.

As usual, the truck remained on Sycamore as it crossed Old Route 66. It went five more blocks before driving around Roosevelt Park to Isotopes Park, the baseball stadium where the minor league team plays. This was becoming an interesting turn of events. We could see across the field another truck pulling into the parking lot just before Philip turned. We stopped on the street near a playground where others parents had parked. It would have been way too obvious if we had pulled into the empty parking lot too.

Michelle quickly grabbed the binoculars again while I grabbed my camera and began clicking picture after picture, snapping as quickly as the camera would allow. Click after click after click could be heard in the silence of our car. Even Lucy sat silently waiting to be let out to run around in the open field.

Both drivers got out of their trucks and exchanged forty

or more cases of beverages. They looked almost identical with their uniforms. The second driver was the same height as Phillip. His hair was slighter shorter and darker, but they both had muscular arms and slim faces. He was wearing dark black work boots. They could have been brothers.

"Caroline," Michelle said as she broke the silence that seemed to have last ten minutes, "I think you're right. I think something unusual is going on here."

"Can you make out the number on the front of the other truck?" I asked Michelle.

"It has the Mexican flag that you were telling me about. I know the first two numbers are 0 - 5," Michelle continued. "It's hard to see since the other driver is standing in front of his truck now. Wait a second. 0 - 5 - 3. Just move over a little bit please," Michelle whispered as if they could hear her. "0-5-3-1-7-1," Michelle exclaimed with excitement. Even Lucy yelped when she heard the excitement of Michelle's voice. "Is that the same number?" she asked.

"It sure is Michelle, or should I call you Quinn?" I asked with a laugh. "That's the actual truck that was on location when Cal disappeared," I claimed.

Lucy started to whimper a little. It was time for a quick break. I jumped out of the truck and quickly opened the back door where Lucy jumped onto the sidewalk. She ran into the grass, squatted, and was wagging her tail again in no time. She and I were hidden behind the truck so the men couldn't see us. Even if they did notice us, we were so far away that they wouldn't be able to identify us. The two men spoke for two more minutes before returning to their seats. It was just long enough time for Lucy to jump out and get back into the truck. "We are going on a journey," I told Lucy as I shut the door behind her.

"You know, Caroline, I've never been a detective before," Michelle chuckled when I shut my door. "Don't you think we should follow the Mexican truck instead? It's Saturday and I don't have anything better to do, until tonight anyway. We could follow him for a while and see where it leads us."

Chapter Seven
GOING FOR A RIDE

"How much time did you say you needed to get ready for your date?" I asked Michelle almost three hours into our trip. We left the park at 8:20 am and it was now 11:15 am. The Rio-Cola truck had not made a single stop. We were heading straight down Highway 25 towards El Paso. The Highway 10 interchange, just south of Las Cruces, that lead into El Paso was about ten miles ahead.

"I just need a half hour to get ready and a half hour to get back down town," Michelle said. "It would be nice if I could get back home no later than 5:30 pm."

"If we go all the way into El Paso, we will barely have enough time to make it back with one stop. We can fill the tank and grab a quick bite to eat," I calculated.

Michelle pondered that statement for a moment before asking, "Will we have any time at all to see what he might be doing in El Paso? Or, will we need to turn around immediately and head back?"

"If we don't have any delays, it should allow us a half hour to see where he goes," I explained to Michelle.

"I just don't want to be late for my date," Michelle insisted.

"I think you'll have plenty of time to get ready and drive

downtown," I reassured my friend.

We had spent the past several hours talking about all the different possibilities of our scenario as Lucy slept in the back seat. We talked about drug laundering, espionage, and, of course, kidnapping. We even talked about the upcoming routes that the truck could follow, and which one was probably the most likely route that it would take. It didn't matter what we spoke about, each scenario was followed with a "what if" by one of us.

"Don't you think the driver looks like a young George Harrison?" I asked Michelle after she showed me some of the close up pictures that I had taken.

"George who?" Michelle asked in response.

"You know, George Harrison, from the Beatles. He reminds me of pictures I've seen of George Harrison when he was in his twenties," I explained.

"That's way before my time. The only Harrison he reminds me of is Harrison Ford," Michelle responded back. "He's tall, thin, muscular, and has a cute face. Let's nickname him Harrison, after both of them," Michelle decided.

"That works for me," I agreed. "I always liked the name Harrison even though I'm not sure if this Harrison is clean or shady."

Harrison could take highway 10 into El Paso, stay on highway 10 as it veered southwest towards San Antonio, or he could cross the border. Our guts kept telling us that he would cross the border. The Mexican flag meant something or it wouldn't be on the truck. We anxiously counted down each mile, as we got closer to the interchange.

"I can't believe he hasn't stopped yet," Michelle said as she yawned. "It must be a guy-thing because any woman I know would have stopped by now," she continued.

"I agree. I wish he would stop soon because I need to use the restroom. I'm not sure how much longer I can hold out," I commented.

Michelle yawned a few more times, and then to our surprise, Harrison exited the highway at the Mesilla Valley Mall exit, two stops prior to the interchange. If he were stopping only for lunch, this would be the perfect exit. There were several gas stations and a dozen restaurants that we could choose. We would go wherever Harrison didn't go. The Rio-Cola truck was big enough to see across any parking lot, so it would be easy to keep an eye on it.

We kept our distance as we pulled off the highway behind Harrison. There were at least a dozen vehicles between us. He turned towards the mall parking lot, and headed towards Five Guys.

"Okay, Caroline, what's the plan?" Michelle asked.

"Let's quickly fill up with gas and grab some snacks and a sandwich at the gas station. Then we can pull behind some cars in the parking lot and wait for him. When he's ready to roll, we can follow behind again," she said.

"We can do that," Michelle said, "but don't you want to get a better look at his truck?"

"What?" I asked.

"Let's get the gas and snacks, and if there's enough time, I will let you know part two of the plan," she said. "We didn't drive all this way for nothing."

After filling up with gas and snacks, we drove through the mall parking lot where it was easy to see that Five Guys had a long line of customers. Harrison was still standing behind an older couple. Michelle then explained her plan in detail. We would need the help of Lucy to pull this one off.

The nice thing about Lucy is that she was properly trained to use her dog run which is full of pea gravel. If she's not at home, she will go in the grass at the park. When there is only a parking lot for her to use, she usually tries to find some sort of gravel. The trees, bordering the parking lot, were landscaped with rocks, and they happened to be next to where Harrison parked the truck. He was directly in front of Five Guys along the mall side of the street since his truck was too big to pull into the Five Guys parking lot. Lucy would want to go near the trees since there isn't any grass nearby.

"So, let me get this straight," I said to Michelle. "You want me to go up to the truck and lift up each door to see what kind of cola he has in each bin, or to see if I find anything suspicious? And, if he happens to come outside while I'm looking in his truck, you will send Lucy over to him as if she is a runaway dog that got lose from you?"

"Yea," she responded. We know that the beverages that were exchanged earlier came from the driver's side of both trucks. The guys just lifted the doors. They weren't locked. The trucks were facing the opposite direction of one another. According to the picture you showed me of the three trucks parked at the light, it's the passenger side of the truck that was near the sidewalk when Cal disappeared. Wouldn't that be the side of the truck you want to see?" Michelle explained. "So, what are you waiting for? Go, before it's too late."

Caroline quickly walked up to the truck hoping no one would question her. She began lifting the doors one by one. Michelle took Lucy on leash to the front of the restaurant. She stopped by the trees first where Lucy began sniffing before squatting, and then Michelle continued to walk her around the outskirts of the parking lot. Lucy was thrilled to be out of the truck.

I had just looked into the last bay of the truck when I heard a loud familiar voice, "Lucy, Lucy, come back here," Michelle was shouting. I wasn't sure if I should run around the front of the truck to retrieve my dog or run back to hide behind some cars. As much as I wanted to get my dog back, I thought I better head back to my truck. I could always pull my Land Rover around and let Lucy jump in.

I turned and walked over to my truck, climbed in, and then backed slowly out of the parking spot, looking to make sure no one was following me. I was paranoid that someone may have seen me sneaking around the truck. I then drove towards the restaurant hoping to park behind a pickup truck. Fortunately for me, there was one right as I pulled in keeping my vehicle hidden from Harrison.

It was then, when I peered through the windows of two other vehicles, that my mouth fell open. I sat steering with the sight of something I had never seen before with Lucy. She had a hamburger and its wrapper drooling out of her mouth. She was sitting quietly on the ground next to Michelle who was fervently trying to apologize for Lucy's actions. Lucy's ravenous appetite or keen smell for that hamburger had overcome all control.

From my perspective, it looked like Lucy had just snatched Harrison's hamburger right out of his hand, the bag and all.

I sat there as I watched Harrison, still holding onto another Five Guy's brown bag, climb up into his truck and shut the door. I could hear Michelle say once more that she was so sorry as he pulled away. She just stood there, now with Lucy's leash in hand, waiting for him to leave.

Once he turned the corner, I swiftly pulled up next to my friends. "Jump in," I said, and then I burst out laughing. "I'm not sure that was part of your plan, Michelle, but it certainly worked," I continued.

"Oh my word, can you believe that?" Michelle blurted out. "Did you see what Lucy just did?"

"I just saw her chomping her lips as she ate the last few bites of the burger with the paper still hanging from her mouth. And, of course, I saw you desperately trying to apologize," I answered.

"Every thing was fine, going as planned, until Harrison walked through the parking lot past the last row of cars. Before I knew it, Lucy tugged so hard that I dropped her leash as she ran towards him. She bit into the closest bag she could find, and snatched it right out of his hands," Michelle expounded. "I couldn't stop her. She just went."

"So, how mad was he?" I asked. "He waited in line for a long time. He must have been furious with you," I said with a chuckle.

"Actually, Harrison was rather nice to me. He accepted my apology, and said that he understood since he has a couple of dogs himself. I told him that I was dog sitting for a friend, and

I had no idea that she would take off across the parking lot. He then said that it was no big deal. They had messed up on his order, and had to remake his hamburger. Since they couldn't sell the first one, they gave it to him anyway. He told me that he was going to throw it away, but didn't want to do it in front of them," Michelle explained. "Lucy was lucky that she grabbed the bag out of his left hand instead of his right hand. It was the burger he had planned to toss."

We could see the Rio-Cola truck pick up speed as it entered the on ramp of the highway. We were stopped at the light on the other side of the bridge. It didn't take long for us to find Harrison again after we passed the traffic where the highway merged into Highway 10. We were now only thirty-five minutes from the border. We had decided earlier in the day that no matter what happened, we would turn around no later than 1:00 pm. We didn't want Michelle to be late for her date. Philip might be able to provide us with additional clues.

"You didn't have any plans for today, did you, Michelle?" I asked while we were eating our sandwiches and chips. "I'm sorry if I ruined your plans. I just never thought the day would end up like this," I continued. "I was planning to clean the pool so everyone could swim at the party tomorrow. I guess I'll have to do that tomorrow morning now."

This definitely has been more exciting than anything I would have done at home so don't worry about it. I just hope I'm not too tired for tonight's date," Michelle said as she leaned her head back for a brief moment. "Maybe I can take a short nap on our way back."

Michelle and I were anxious after we crossed the state

line into Texas. We could see the Franklin Mountains on our left and knew the city would rise out of the sky shortly if we continued to look straight down the highway. El Paso was on the edge of the Rio Grande River, which separated it from the Mexican border. The brown foothills were now on our left, and plains of wild yellow roses scattered the desert floor on our right. Within minutes, we were engulfed in a sea of traffic, and constantly changing lanes to keep up with the flow. It seemed like we blinked, and the traffic appeared. The first of two exits was fast approaching that would easily lead a traveler to the border. The question remained, "Would Harrison exit the highway and head for the border, or not?"

The highway took a ninety-degree turn to the east as it continued through town. Factories surrounded us and high-rise buildings could be seen about a half-mile away. Harrison stayed on the highway as we rounded the bend. We were relieved. He didn't exit. We continued through the heavy traffic. He still had another opportunity to exit and cross over into Mexico.

Oncoming traffic was merging onto the highway just before the last exit that would lead towards the border. Harrison had been driving in the far right hand lane, but then he merged into the middle lane just when we thought he might exit. He was making room for the approaching cars.

"Not only is he good looking, but he's a polite driver too," Michelle remarked. "He actually got over so those cars could enter the highway. That doesn't happen often."

"Well, I'm relieved," I said. "I don't know why though. "What's the difference if he heads towards San Antonio or crosses the border? It still doesn't tell us anything about where he is going." I added. "If you hadn't made a date, we could keep following him."

"I know, but I didn't even realize there were two different trucks until this morning," Michelle responded. "Do you want me to cancel the date?"

"No, because Phillip will probably never ask you out again. This could be our only chance to find out more information about Cal's whereabouts or disappearance," I said. "I need to find out what happens during the week. There's no way that Harrison is making this trip every day. And, if Phillip meets a truck there every day, then maybe there are more trucks. Next time, we should probably pack our bags and plan to stay over night."

"Next time, give me a warning," Michelle uttered as we exited the highway to head back north. Harrison had passed through El Paso and clearly was not stopping anywhere around here. "And, maybe we will know what to look for the next time too," she said.

I then spent the next several minutes telling her about the truck. I had completely forgotten to tell Michelle about it when we were distracted by Lucy. The truck had six different bays with sidetrack doors that I lifted by pulling up on the leather strap that was attached to the bottom of each door. The doors were a little heavier than I expected, but I only needed to open each one a few feet to see inside.

I first opened the end one near the back of the truck. It was completely full of Sprite and Fresca. Then I opened the two shorter doors above the back wheels. Both of those were full of different types of Powerade. It was the fourth door, the one that has Cola spelled on it that surprised me. The door itself lifted much easier than the other three doors that I had already lifted. The door track itself was slightly wider and smoother. It didn't make a sound when I opened it. The other doors rattled a little bit and were harder to lift. The door glided up as if it were coated in butter.

As I pulled up on the leather strap, I was expecting to find Rio-Cola or a diet version of it, but to my astonishment, the alcove was empty. It was vacant. I didn't even see a spec of dust. It was clean as if it had recently been washed. I quickly put that door down. My heart pounded even faster after I lifted that door. There was enough room for four or five average size men to fit in there.

I was fearful to open the next two doors, but knew I needed to see inside of them. I swung the fifth door up and found case after case of Slim Cola and Rio-Cola Zero. That's what I expected to see every time I lifted the other doors. It was my final door on the passenger side of the truck, and I was expecting to hear Lucy's bark at any time now, but as I lifted the door it was the sound of Michelle's scream that I heard echoing through the air. I had only lifted the door about three feet high when I quickly pulled it back down. The bottom stack of beverages was Rio-Cola Life with a green and white label rather than the standard red and white.

"Rio-Cola Life," I had asked Michelle, "Have you ever heard of it before?"

"Of course, I have heard about it. I'm a teacher. I hear about everything," Michelle responded. "Other than an empty bay and the nicer door glides, there wasn't anything else you noticed about the truck, right Caroline?"

"No, I didn't see anything else that would raise an eyebrow," I commented.

"An empty bay could mean anything," Michelle added. "I don't think we should jump to any conclusions, but keep that information tucked in the back of our minds. You never know if it might lead to another clue."

I then took a drink of my Pepsi, and turned the music on low. We were heading home, driving north through El Paso again, when Michelle rolled her long sleeve shirt up into a ball to use as a pillow. When I looked over again, she was fast asleep. I had a lot to think about now too. What did all of this mean?

Chapter Eight
THE DATE

Half perched on the wooden frame stool, sat a cowboy with long flowing hair at the bar of the Brazilian grill. His right boot rested comfortably on the riser while his left leg dangled down to the floor showcasing his unforgettable boots. He wore his jeans tight, and his shirt and jacket even tighter. A slanted smile crossed his face when he turned to see a woman approaching him. His face remained unshaven with whiskers just long enough to feel rough to the touch. His tall Pilsner glass was half full. He looked down at the glass, then turned again and lifted his head in speechless wonderment.

She came walking through the doors full of confidence and grace. Her long blonde curls swayed with each step as she approached the counter. Her heals were high, and her blue dress modestly outlined her sexy body and defined legs. At first glance, anyone would think she was a model. Very few people would ever speculate that she was a teacher and competitive cyclist.

A blistering thump in her heart could be felt as she walked closer to him. Questions were swirling through her mind faster than a gust of wind. Could she be herself around him knowing that she spent the entire day spying on him and Harrison? Could he be trusted? Would she be able to restrain herself from saying something she shouldn't? How would this night end?

The restaurant was crowded. It was a Saturday night. The sounds of laughter, music, and clinging dishes could be heard, but in that moment there was silence as if time stood still. Her grand entrance made heads turn, yet she was oblivious to it all. She was focused on a premonition that she had not seen, touched, or felt ever before. She did not know why, but she was being lured to a perplexing man like lodestone attracting iron. It was an unstoppable attraction.

There were two things about Michelle that everyone knew. She was not shy nor did she ever lack words to speak. She was used to being the center of attention whether it was in the classroom or on a podium accepting an award. She was the friend that everyone wanted to be, and the girlfriend that most men wanted on their side. Why she would be attracted to a delivery driver was as much a mystery to her as he was mystifying.

This was the first time that Michelle stepped foot into a restaurant alone with another man in two years. Her fiancé had left on a business trip to Europe all those months ago. He was scheduled to be gone for two weeks, before arriving in Brussels where he would meet a colleague before traveling to Zurich. The two weeks turned into three weeks that then turned into four. The last she heard, he had settled in Livorno, Italy with no plans for a return trip home anytime soon.

"You clean up well, Cowboy," Michelle said as Phillip stood up, placed his hands on her shoulders and leaned forward to kiss her on the cheek.

"I see you are a woman of your word," he responded

back. "I was hoping I wouldn't have to finish this draft by my-self. Our table should be ready in a moment or two."

She sat down beside him. The fragrance of his cologne still lingered in her hair. It had been a long time since she had been close enough to any man to smell his manliness. Michael Kors was the first name that popped into her head.

"MK?" she asked.

"What?" he responded.

"Michael Kors?" she asked again.

"Oh yes," he replied somewhat surprised that she knew in just a brief moment the cologne he wore.

"I wasn't sure," Michelle continued. "I thought it might have been Giorgio Armani. It's been a long time."

"Not a bad guess for someone who wasn't too sure," he answered again.

By now the bartender had already motioned to Michelle, asking if she wanted a drink. What she really wanted was a glass of White Zinfandel, but she knew she couldn't pass up one of their specialty drinks.

After a slight deliberation, Michelle responded, "a Tuca-nos with rum, please."

"Malibu all right?" the bartender questioned.

"Yes, that's fine," she said as she turned to look into the Mediterranean blue eyes of her new friend.

"So my queen prefers irresistible passion and pineapple tonight?" Phillip asked keenly studying his new acquaintance, while referencing some of the ingredients of her drink.

"Queen?" Michelle responded.

"If I do recall correctly, madam, you referred to yourself

as Quinn early this morning. If that is correct, are you not a queen?" he proceeded to say trying to maintain his charm. I believe that Quinton is an old English version of queen.

"Awe, you're an English scholar as well as a delivery driver?" Michelle asked cunningly.

Phillip replied slowly, deliberately pausing as he spoke. "Perhaps. I might know a little something about English... and Spanish... and French."

Michelle was amused. Her cowboy was sophisticated, an element she did not expect coming from a Rio-Cola truck driver. "Yes, then," she said pausing just long enough to emphasize her response. "The queen actually prefers wine; not only tonight, but on most nights," she said as the corner of her lips sustained her whimsical smile. "But, sweet mango, papaya, pineapple, and ice cream will better quench my thirst on this hot evening."

"I thought you might prefer brew. That's what you picked up this morning," he pointed out.

"That's for the Super Bowl tomorrow," Michelle quickly responded.

"Oh, yes, I'm sure you are going to drink a twelve pack by yourself," he said chuckling as the hostess approached.

"Mr. Terric, your table is ready.

The couple was taken to a table near the back of the restaurant where the lights were dimmed slightly lower than the main corridor and bar. It was much quieter there allowing their conversation to flow free of other audible distractions.

"Are you ready for the Churrasco?" Phillip asked Michelle. "That's what this place is all about, isn't it?" he asked as she glanced a second time through the menu.

Michelle sighed. "With one skewer, I'm practically done eating," she said still grinning from the charge she was experiencing simply by being with the cowboy. "I love their Sea Scallop Skewer," Michelle announced. "And, I love their Salad Festival. It's by far the best salad bar around."

"Oh, come on," Phillip protested. "Where's your adventure?"

"I'll meet you halfway. I'll try everything but the chicken hearts with the Churrasco, if you order an Ipanema. You can have a beer anytime. Their signatures drinks are unforgettable though."

"Deal," Phillip said reaching across the table to take Michelle's hand. She thought he was simply closing the deal with a handshake. Instead, she was surprised when he lifted her hand for a kiss.

Moments after returning from the salad bar, the Churrasco began when James, the head chef and meat server appeared at their table with a sample of Peru, a fancy name for turkey wrapped in bacon.

The couple talked and laughed for three hours, completely unaware that the tables around them were slowly losing the voices that had echoed around them all evening. Michelle was still careful not to say or ask anything that could potentially be harmful to her or Caroline, but she certainly had shared some intimate things about herself that she would never share on a first date. She talked about her love for teaching, the children in her classroom, and her obsession with cycling. He was impressed.

Michelle had waited all evening to inquire about Phillip's job, and then she finally said, "So, tell me, Phillip, why does a ravishing English scholar cowboy like you work as a delivery driver?"

"It will take another three hours for me to answer that question. We'll have to finish this date elsewhere or you'll have to go out again with me," he replied. "I'll give you a brief version for now. I needed a job where I could work from six in the morning until one in the afternoon. My brother got the job for me. He's the plant manager of the distribution center in El Paso. He used to work here, but took a promotion and moved down there about three years ago."

"Awe, like a progressive dinner you are suggesting a progressive date?" Michelle responded.

"Perhaps," Phillip chuckled.

"What's your brother's name?" Michelle then asked. "You didn't mention him earlier."

"Henry. He's two years older than me. People used to say that we looked like twins growing up. I don't think so. He's got dark brown hair that often looks black in the dark of the night and very dark chocolate eyes. He looks like our mother. I look like my dad."

"Are they ever going to stop serving me Churrasco? I am so full," Phillip continued. James, had made countless trips to their table, slicing off a piece of top sirloin, garlic Parmesan beef, Brazilian sausage, and countless other specialty meats. Not only had he cooked them to perfection, but he also had tongue-twisting names for each of them as well.

"Not unless you show them it's time to stop," Michelle

laughed. "Do you see that green Tucanos Cue that you have been fiddling with for the past half hour?"

"Yes," he said looking down at the three-color gadget in his hands.

"You have kept the green side up this entire time. When you want the Churrasco to stop, you must place the red side up. It's a rather simple concept," she added laughing hysterically now. "I've been waiting to see how long it would take for you to figure it out."

"I completely forgot that I needed to turn it upside down. I guess I have been a little distracted tonight," he said trying to maintain his composure.

"Awe, I see you have outlasted all the other men in the restaurant tonight," James said as he inquired one last time before Phillip agreed he had eaten too much.

"I didn't want to miss out on your Frango Picante or your grilled Abacaxi," Phillip replied trying to impress his date with the Brazilian names of spicy barbeque chicken and grilled pineapple.

"That's my job not to disappoint you or let you miss out on anything," James replied with a chuckle.

"It was all delicious and I honestly don't know which cut was my favorite," Phillip complimented the chef. "It was all fabulous."

"Well, thank you," James said before retreating back to the kitchen.

Unlike most restaurants that feature an individual choice of meat, Tucanos features fourteen varieties of Brazilian favorites along with grilled vegetables that are served directly to your table as they come off the grill. A person can select all of them or even order specialty skewers of seafood.

"Caroline, wake up," Michelle said as she tapped her friend on the shoulder.

Hidden around the corner in a nook, Caroline was lounging comfortably in a Jacques Garcia Atrium chair in a nearby hotel lobby, just a half a block away from Tucanos, in the opposite direction of the bus station across the street. The book she had been reading, turned spine up with a few pages wrinkled from the book's fall, was resting near her feet. A bookmarker, formed in the shape of a hot air balloon, had floated to the floor next to the book.

This was very unlike Caroline to fall asleep in a public place. She must have been exhausted from a day's worth of driving. She had spent most of the evening by herself in Mas Tapas Y Vino, devouring the grilled flatiron steak. An older gentleman from the bar had sent her a drink since she was eating alone, but she refused to accept it. She was the security plan for Michelle, if Phillip proved to be shady. She was sure Michelle would have a few drinks too. Unlike many adults, the two friends always drove responsibly.

"Oh, Quinn," I said as I rolled my eyes opened. I then looked around, hoping no one had noticed that I was asleep. "I can't believe I actually fell asleep." I then looked down on my cell to see the time. It was only eleven.

"How did it go?" I asked as Michelle and I began to walk to my car. I could tell that Michelle really liked this guy. I had not seen her so excited about a date in years.

"He is so good looking, Caroline, and sophisticated and

fun. I don't know what a delivery driver is supposed to be like, but this guy is no typical driver. He seems like he really has his act together. There isn't a thing I don't like about him."

"Did you learn anything about Harrison?" I asked.

"Yes, Harrison is actually Henry, Phillip's older brother," Michelle began to explain. "He is the supervisor of the plant in El Paso. He moved down there about three years ago. Philip said that he needed a job where he could work from six in the morning till one in the afternoon. Henry helped him get this job. He said the story was too long to share tonight, but he would tell me about it later."

"Did he say where he lives," I asked.

"No. I didn't want to bring that topic up. We talked about our child hoods and the things we like. We talked a long time about our favorite foods, music and sports. I also told him about school and my students. We talked a little about cycling. We just talked. I can't remember everything since we were there for so long. He was just so charming. I just wanted to take him home with me."

"Did he tell you his last name," I then asked.

"No," Michelle responded, but when our table was ready the hostess came up to us and said, 'Mr. Terric, you're table is ready.'"

"That's great, Michelle. Maybe we can do our own little research," I said.

"I can get a background check on them from school," Michelle said. "All of our volunteers have to be approved so I will submit their names as if they are volunteers. I don't know of anyone who hasn't been approved.

"Will you actually get a report on them?" I inquired.

"No one ever pulls the report, but there is a place in the software that allows us to pull a report if we think it's needed. There's only one time that I remember anyone ever doing it. One of the young science teachers had a crush on one of the divorced moms. He met her at the parent/student conferences. He waited until the end of the school year because he didn't want rumors to fly. He pulled her report to see where she worked. Then he conveniently found an excuse to be in the neighborhood when she was getting off work. Sure enough, she came out of work just as he was walking by. They went on a few dates. I haven't kept up on the story though. I don't see that teacher very often."

There was less traffic on the road at this time of night, so the drive back to Michelle's house went fast. Both ladies were excited about this new romantic love that Michelle stumbled upon. Neither expected this day or evening to turn out as it did. Their minds and Michelle's heart were inflamed with a burning to know more about these brothers.

"Anything else?" I asked Michelle just before we turned onto the street towards her house.

"Well, he likes my name Quinn," Michelle explained. "He was surprised to see me order a glass of wine instead of beer tonight since I bought the beer this morning. I told him it was for a Super Bowl party. I think he was hoping I would invite him to the party. Oh, he also wanted to walk me to my car when we were leaving too."

"What did you tell him?" I asked eagerly hoping to hear the play by play.

Michelle was tired and quickly losing her energy now. She probably had one too many drinks as well. She was lacking the normal detail she typically gives when story telling. She tried to explain. "Well, as we stood up to leave, he grabbed my hand as if we had been together before. We then walked out the front door and stopped. I could tell he wanted to kiss me, but I turned away, pretending that I don't kiss on the first date. I so wanted to kiss him, Caroline, but I knew I shouldn't. Too much is at stake with you. He then asked to walk me to my car. I simply told him, 'no, not tonight.'

"So, you both just walked your separate ways" I questioned as I turned into Michelle's driveway.

"I started walking away. After about twenty steps, I stopped and turned around and called his name. He was still standing there just watching me walk away. I said I forgot to say 'thank you.' I quickly ran up to him and when I was two steps away, he grabbed my arm and swung me close to him. I kissed him as he held me tight, wrapped in the strength of his arms. I melted."

He asked if he could call me. I told him most definitely, 'yes.' I then came straight to the hotel as we had planned only to find you asleep in the corner. I stood watching you sleep for almost five minutes before I woke you up. I hope you don't hate me, Caroline."

"It sounds like you stood there for five minutes because you could still feel the warmth of his kiss on your lips," I smarted back.

"I'm sorry Caroline. Can we just talk tomorrow? I'm really tired now. I actually feel a headache coming on. Hey, thanks for the ride and for waiting around for me. I'll be over to help set up. I'll call when I wake up," she said as she walked towards her front door.

I sat in her driveway for several minutes after she unlocked the door and walked inside. I was numb. I wanted to be happy for Michelle, but the Terric brothers were my main suspects right now. How could they be trusted? Why would they need to trade cases of coke? It just didn't make any sense to me. I sure hope Michelle hasn't found another heart breaker.

I hope I don't forget to tell Michelle about my discovery tonight either. After eating dinner at the restaurant, I scrolled through the pictures I took earlier today of the brothers and compared them to the driver who drove the Rio-Cola truck on that dreadful morning. He was a different guy. At first glance, they all look alike. They easily could be mistaken for triplets.

Chapter Nine
THE PARTY

The sun crested above the distant mountains a few minutes after seven this morning. The daybreak air was cool, but refreshing as I opened the door for Lucy. She quickly ran outside, invigorated by the smells and breeze of the outdoors and by the need to relieve her self. I wanted to climb back into bed. I undoubtedly did not get enough sleep last night, but I knew the pool needed cleaned for my big event.

I stuck my head out the door as I watched Lucy turn the corner, headed for her dog run. The sun was warm against my face. I could hear three birds chirp back and forth. It had been a long time since I had stopped long enough to listen to the birds. A green kingfisher and yellow-bellied bird flew over the pool while a lark perched on the pool fence. On numerous occasions, I had seen a blue-throated hummingbird back along the wall of flowering vines, but it was too early for him to be out this morning.

In just a few short hours, the house would be full of chatter and laughter, as in the days prior to Cal's disappearance. The temperatures were warmer than previous winters in Albuquerque, so I was thrilled that the high would reach seventy-three degrees. This would be perfect for children aching to swim outdoors in a pool during the winter. The water was warmer than yesterday. I had turned the pool heater up to eighty-two degrees.

It occurred to me while I was testing the water that most pool owners close their pools during the winter months around here. Maybe it was the milder temperatures or the fact that the previous homeowners were trying to showcase their property so they kept it open this year. It didn't bother me one bit that the pool was still open. It allowed me the chance to enjoy my new back yard with the fully functional pool.

A pool shed housed a twelve-month supply of chemicals and cleaners that would be needed to maintain a perfectly balanced pool. Specific instructions with photographs were compiled together in a binder along with a water log. I never expected this kind of detail for the pool. Someone must have felt it necessary in teaching a novice the quirks of this pool. I don't know if professionals routinely cleaned the pool, but I purchased a six-month learner's package where a professional would come out to my house once each month to test the waters and teach me the necessary skills needed for me to enjoy my pool. The winterizing aspect was the final lesson.

This was only the fourth time that I had cleaned the pool since I moved in. All of my leaf falling trees were on the backside of my property which left very little opportunity for leaves and debris to fall into the pool. The waterfall and pumps circulated the water allowing any unwanted rubbish to collect in a basket. A creepy crawling pool cleaner automatically attached to the pool bottom and walls, suctioning and dispensing pool dust from the chemicals. It limited my time to a minimal for cleaning. Without even changing out of my nigh clothes, I threw on my Chicago Bears sweatshirt and tackled the project quickly.

To give all the kids ample time to swim prior to the start of the big game, a three o'clock start was established. This was perfect for families with younger children too because they could swim first and leave after half time. The grilling of burgers and brats would start around four thirty. There would be plenty of snacks for everyone to munch if they couldn't wait till dinner.

After cleaning the pool, I made a double batch of chocolate oatmeal cookies before Michelle arrived. They were quick and easy to make, and didn't require any baking. I always add peanut butter to them which creates a creamier chocolate peanut buttery taste. By the time Michelle showed up, I had already snacked on cheese and crackers, fresh yellow peppers with dip, carrots, and the cookies.

It was almost one o'clock now when the front door bell rang. It was Michelle, standing with her arms full of food. She brought guacamole chip dip, chips, and a Firehouse Sub bag that dangled down from her arm. "Are you hungry?" Michelle asked when I opened the door. "I'm starving and can't wait until dinner. I got a sandwich for you too. I put in a thirty-eight mile ride this morning since I couldn't ride yesterday."

"Hi Michelle," I said when she entered. "Let's put the dip in the refrigerator for now," as I took it from her. "I'll just have a few bites of the sandwich. I've been munching all morning," I told her. "You seem all chipper today," I said as we sat down to eat.

"Well, a little sleep and ibuprofen will do wonders," Michelle responded with an oversized smile still pasted to her cheeks.

"You just can't stop thinking about him, can you? I asked.

"I'm so sorry Caroline. I didn't try to hurt you. I never expected him to be this incredible. He's more than just a delivery driver. I honestly thought I might be able to learn something from him that might help with your investigation. I'm just really confused right now. He seems genuine and honest. I had a great first date and we plan to go out again," she blurted, still chewing on her food.

"Has he called you yet?" I asked.

"No, but he will. I'm sure of that," she responded again. She then looked at her phone before finishing her sandwich. "What can I do to help?"

"I think everything is set except the drinks. We need to fill the Pepsi cooler with ice, then add the drinks," I explained. "It's out on the patio."

While visiting my parents a few years ago, I brought an old fashion metal cooler back to Albuquerque with me. They frequently used it in previous years, but had not been entertaining as much recently. They decided it was time for a springcleaning. This made the donation list. When Cal and I lived in town, I kept the cooler in the garage because I didn't have a good place for it in our small back yard. The cafe area here is a perfect place for it now. It's ideal. It's on wheels and mounted on metal brackets about two feet off the ground. A built-in bottle opener on the left side makes opening bottles easy.

Michelle followed me to the butler pantry just inside the back door. This was so much easier than the other house, no more hiking back and forth from the garage to the extra refrigerator. She grabbed a bag of ice while I took a twelve pack in one hand and Rio-Cola in the other. We stepped outside to the cooler where we neatly placed the drinks on ice. Michelle went back for some bottled water and juice boxes while I strolled over to the built-in wine cooler that was also located inside the pantry.

I had known for years that Michelle was a white wine fan so I pulled out three of her favorites; Barefoot Riesling, River Road Chardonnay, and Iron Mountain White Zinfandel. A Norton Cabernet Sauvignon, Sutter Home Zinfandel, and Kilikanoon Shiraz were my choice of reds. Each of the bottles was carefully placed in a large metal bowl with ice waiting for guests to arrive.

After everything was in place, drinks chilling on ice, and food prepped, Michelle and I sat out by the pool to relax. I handed her a bottle of cold water, only to hear a sarcastic tone penetrate through her vocal chords. Apparently, I had not been sensitive enough to catch her vibes.

"Seriously, Caroline," she said standing up and walking back to the refrigerator. "A bottle of water? I just went on a 38-mile bike ride this morning. Do you realize how much water I have already had for the day?" Without giving me a chance to respond, she continued, "I want to talk about last night, and it just doesn't seem right to do that with a plastic bottle of water in my hand."

"Well, I didn't think you would want to start drinking so early today," I piped back. "Besides, if I recall, you did have your fair share of beverages last night."

"Let's compromise then," she said as she grabbed hard

lemonade from the refrigerator.

I took a wine cooler as we head back outside before the intrusion of friends arrived. We felt like we had just survived two weeks of nonstop action, when it had only been two days, and the party had not even begun yet.

"I just want to feel love again," Michelle began to explain as she talked about her time last night with Phillip. "It has taken me all these months to get over the devastation of Alex leaving me. He left three months before our wedding. I never thought I could love again, Caroline. But, last night, everything changed. In that one moment when our eyes met again for the first time as I walked across the floor to where he was sitting at the bar, I felt a shiver run through my entire body. I physically felt his love in that moment as if lighting struck and melted my fears. His sex appeal alone drew me towards him, but then I discovered the depth of his soul and knew there was so much more to him."

"I'm happy for you Michelle. I really am. I just don't know if we can trust him fully yet," I tried to explain. "It was just twenty four hours ago that he was our main suspect in a crime that has been left unsolved."

"I know you are trying to protect me, Caroline. I'm sorry I even brought it up. I know how shattered your life has been the past several months. I have just never felt this way before, ever… not even with Alex. I thought I loved him. We had two great years together. I wanted to spend the rest of my life with him. Then he just left, using his trip as an excuse. He didn't even say goodbye to me. I hated him at first, and every time someone tried to set me up on a date, I couldn't do it. I compared everyone to Alex. I have had such a hard time getting over him. Then out of the blue, you asked me to go with you yesterday. I could never have dreamt for the day to be one of adventure, yet alone one full of romance. The connection I felt with Phillip last night was unlike any I have ever experienced before. I just can't stop thinking about him. It's hard to describe. It's like we always loved one another. It was a natural kind of love where there were no boundaries, and nothing being sought in return. Was it like that when you first met Calvin?"

"Michelle, I can't even begin to say how much you mean to me. I couldn't have gotten through this mess without you. And, even though I am hurting, and so desperately miss Calvin, don't ever feel like you can't talk to me about your own love life. That's what best friends do. I know my situation is different than yours because Alex deliberately walked out on you. In my heart, I don't believe that is what Cal did to me. After seeing that truck yesterday, I still think he was kidnapped. The pain never ends. I think about him constantly. I just don't understand why there hasn't been a ransom note and no one has come forth asking for money. To answer your question, yes, it was like that with Cal. You remember. If it weren't for you, we never would have met."

"I am so hoping Phillip had nothing to do with Calvin's disappearance, Caroline. After talking with him last night, I just can't imagine that he has an ounce of badness in him. If you had not been there waiting for me all night, I'm sure I would have allowed him to walk me to my car. Who knows what would have come next."

"I completely understand your loneliness, Michelle. I

have gone out of my way to stay busy, and Lucy has helped a lot, but there's only so much a dog can do. There is a part of me that will never be happy again. There's a part of me that died. On the surface, I am trying to move on with my life. You know that. This party is to mark a new beginning for me. Even though most of our friends probably think this is a celebration, it's more than just a celebration for me. It's a time to say goodbye to my former life with Cal. You at least have a chance to find love again. I don't. I have to wait at least seven years before the state recognizes his death or disappearance. I try not to think about it that way. When I do, I just miss him more. I miss his kisses. I miss the way he touches me. I miss the way he… you know what I mean. He was a compassionate lover, and now that's all gone too."

"I'm so sorry, Caroline. I never expected this conversation to head down this path. I don't want you to relive what you can't have any more. I was just trying to explain how incredible Phillip made me feel last night. I want that feeling again. And, someday, I hope you can find it again too."

Michelle then reached over to hug me just as Lucy began to bark and run towards the front door.

Felicia and her children were the first guests to arrive. She had not seen the house since I purchased it.

"The floors look great," she said when she first walked in. "It's amazing how much better it looks now," she continued.

"Can we swim now?" Felicia's youngest asked before he even had a chance to walk out back.

"Yes, Julian, you may, but first we need to talk with your mom," I began. "Felicia, do your kids remember your pool rules?" I asked.

"I sure hope they do," she responded. "Kids, what are my three rules?" she then asked.

In unison, they responded, "One. No swimming without an adult. Two. No running on the pool deck. Three. No dunking."

"Do you have any other rules for them?" Felicia then asked me. I didn't have any rules at all. This was the first time anyone would swim in my pool. I wasn't a mom, and never thought about rules until just now. I asked Felicia the rules because I knew she took the kids swimming often, and would probably have a few of her own.

"No, just make sure your mom is out there when you are in the water," I reminded the children.

"Pedro, before you go in the water, please put those Rio-Colas wherever Mrs. Richards would like them," Felicia told her oldest son.

"I have drinks for the kids, Felicia, but if you prefer Rio-Cola over lemonade, you can put them in the cooler outside," I told her and Pedro.

"Oh, yes, we prefer the Cola, Caroline," Felicia remarked. "It taste so much better."

"Do you drink American Cola or Mexican Cola?" I asked

"You know about Mexican Cola?" she responded.

"I don't know much, but I heard that Mexican Cola has a smoother taste because it uses a different sweetener. Is that true?" I then inquired.

"The taste is much smoother. It's like a water slide where the water is uninhabited and runs freely down to the pool. American Rio-Cola, in my opinion, compares to having a fight with a Waterpik. The liquid bounces in every direction creating havoc with your mouth before reaching the back of your throat," Felicia explained.

"Oh, that's a different way of looking at it, Felicia. I never would have thought of that comparison. Can you even buy Mexican Cola here in the States?"

"You can buy it here in Albuquerque, but not very many places sell it. There's a place not too far from our house that sells it."

"Well, if you want to keep it in the refrigerator inside rather than outside where anyone can snatch it, you are welcome to hide it there," I told Pedro who was still standing next to his mother.

"Oh, thank you, Caroline," Felicia expressed.

She and the kids went out to the pool while Michelle and I finished our drinks. Before long, several other families arrived. The party had begun. It was nonstop action. The sound of kids laughing and water splashing was invigorating. My house came alive for the first time since that dreadful day.

When Peter arrived, he volunteered to keep the play list rolling. I showed him where the system was located, and he played every hit imaginable. The kids loved his selections as well as the adults. He had a knack for mixing things up while keeping a steady flow.

"Hey Michelle," I heard Felicia say when I stepped outside to show Josh and Jason my fabulous grill. "Your phone was ringing, so I picked it up to answer it for you, and some guy asked for Quinn. I told him that he had the wrong number. But, here's your phone. You left it over there where you and Caroline were sitting earlier."

Michelle glanced at me and I knew she wanted a private chat, out of earshot of everyone else. "I'll be with you in just a second, Michelle," I said. "I need to talk to the guys first."

I knew it would take awhile to grill enough burgers and brats for almost fifty people, so Joshua and Jason began grill duty almost as soon as they arrived. I was so thankful that they offered to help so I could mingle with everyone. They were grill masters so it didn't take much explaining. Cal, Michelle, and I spent half the year grilling out with these guys and the others from our cycling club. I knew I could rely on them.

Michelle and I managed to make our way through the wave of friends to my room. I shut the door behind me.

"You better call him now," I said. "This is as quiet as it's going to get tonight."

Michelle took a deep breath, "Hi Phillip," she said when he answered the phone.

"This is your phone, Quinn?" the man on the other end asked. I promised myself that I wouldn't call you during your party, but I'm dying to hear your voice again," he said. "When I called this number, someone else answered and said that I had the wrong number," he explained. "I thought you gave me a fake number."

"No, this is the right number. There are a lot of people here and one of my friends thought this was someone else's phone," Michelle fibbed. "I had left it out by the pool."

"Would you like any more company?" he pleaded kindly, hoping he might get an invite.

Caroline had been listening to every word with her ear up to the phone when Michelle held back a screech as she dropped the phone down between her thighs.

"Oh no, Caroline, what do I say?" she whispered hoping he couldn't hear her speak.

Trying to speak as softly as possible, Carolyn replied, "tell him you will call him back in a minute."

"Phillip, can I call you right back? My friend needs me for a second, so I'll call right back. I promise," she fibbed again.

"Okay," the enticing voice replied.

Michelle quickly hung up the phone.

"What do I tell him?" she asked Caroline.

"Tell him no. You are not ready for him to meet your friends yet. Honestly, Michelle, what are you going to tell him when everyone calls you Michelle instead of Quinn? And, what are you going to tell all of our friends- you met him at the grocery store yesterday?

"Oh, I wish it wasn't so complicated," Michelle sighed.

"Well, if you keep seeing him, it's going to get even more complicated," I told her. "I can't imagine what his brother is going to say the first time you meet him. 'Oh, haven't we met before? Yea, you're the lady whose dog stole my hamburger.' I want to be the fly on the wall when that conversation takes place," I said laughing.

Caroline returned to the party, leaving Michelle to fend for herself.

"Hello Phillip. It's me again," Michelle said as she

slouched into Caroline's chaise looking out the window towards the waterfall daydreaming about her new man. "I would love for you come, but I just don't think I'm ready for you to meet my friends yet. Heck, I don't even know why you are a truck driver for Rio-Cola," Michelle added.

Phillip laughed. "I better clear that up for you sometime soon. Maybe we can talk later. Call me when the party is over. Okay?"

"I will. I promise," Michelle said.

"Je tiens à vous voir ce soiree," Phillip then said trying to swoon his new lady friend.

"What?" Michelle asked.

"Quiero ver a ustedes esta noche" Phillip repeated in another language.

"Something about tonight?" Michelle asked. "You want me to call you tonight? Is that it?" Michelle inquired.

"I do want you to call me tonight, but that's not what I said," Phillip informed Michelle.

"Well, I really need to go. Goodbye Phillip."

"Adiós hermosa."

Michelle was grinning again from a new fire that lit her soul.

"Felicia," Michelle asked immediately upon her return to the pool deck, "What does 'Quiero ver a ustedes esta noche' mean?"

Chapter Ten
SPYING AGAIN

Her tongue dangled out of her mouth as she sat waiting to nuzzle the fresh spring smells of the park lawn. Lucy peered through the lightly tinted front window of the Land Rover eyeing the children on the playground. She was anxious to run around and sniff the unfamiliar smells. "No Lucy, you can't do that," Caroline told her dog who was now panting and fogging up the glass.

It was a beautiful Saturday morning, the only day of the week that Lucy could come to the park with Caroline. Lucy acknowledged her owner without having any idea what she had done wrong. She continued to pant. Caroline was preoccupied with her search for her missing husband. After sitting for several minutes, she cracked all the windows about a half-inch to let the air circulate in her truck. The haze quickly dissolved.

Carolyn didn't want anyone else to see that she was using binoculars to spy on other people. Her back was towards the toddlers and parents on the playground. There weren't any other people around that could see unless she stepped out of her truck. Caroline had frequented this park since her discovery of Harrison. It had been the perfect setup for her to park here while waiting for the trucks to arrive.

Caroline had wanted Michelle to go with her to San Antonio when they first discovered Harrison. Now that they know that he actually lives in El Paso, she wasn't sure if would be a good ideal for Michelle to go again since she had seen Phillip every night this week. It had been five weeks since Michelle's first date. Caroline had not officially met him yet due to conflicts with her work schedule. That's what she told Michelle. The truth was she didn't want to meet him, not while she was still investigating him and his brother.

Michelle was so eager for Caroline to meet Phillip that she asked Caroline almost everyday if she could come over to her house after work. When Caroline continuously refused, she scheduled a dinner party for them and a few other friends. She knew Caroline wouldn't be able to decline now. The gathering was planned for next Saturday night.

After the big date, Michelle began referring to Harrison as Henry. Caroline wasn't quite ready to make him her best pal either, so she decided to keep using his nickname. She didn't want to know him personally. He was still a suspect for her. She didn't want to think of him as Phillip's older brother. Until evidence proved otherwise, she wanted to keep it that way. Using his nickname allowed her to stay unemotionally attached since Michelle was quickly growing attached to Phillip.

Michelle pulled the records of both brothers several weeks ago like she had promised. They were both clean. No flags that would prevent either of them from volunteering at the school. Henry had a speeding ticket from eighteen months ago, but other than that they were immaculate. In Michelle's mind, this was the assurance she needed to date Phillip. Caroline, on the other hand, had become untrustworthy of everyone. In her opinion, the reports didn't prove a thing.

As Caroline and Lucy waited, they listened to a morning radio program featuring old classics from the seventies and eighties. Without any forewarning, Take It On The Run, blasted through the speakers. Caroline had not heard this song in years, but she remembered it as if she had heard it just yesterday. Her mom used to play it all the time while cleaning the house while their dad was out. Her mom loved REO Speedwagon, Styx, Journey, Chicago, Foreigner, and Fleetwood Mac. All of their hit songs had been branded into Caroline's memory forever.

When this song came on the radio, Caroline instantly felt at peace; maybe it was the thought of her childhood, or the warm sentiment the music allowed her to feel. Regardless, it placed her in a better mood. She thought the trucks would be arriving in a few minutes. She needed to decide now whether today would be the day she ventured down the highway again. She came prepared.

Last week she had packed a suitcase, snacks, and dog food to keep in the truck for the right moment when she would follow Harrison. Last night she had filled her gas tank again, and this morning she had made sandwiches. A small cooler was just the right size for cold drinks and dog water. When she woke this morning, she wasn't sure if she would make the trip today. She had been invited to attend Felicia's youngest son's birthday party tomorrow afternoon. If everything went well, she thought she could be back in time.

Sure enough, both Rio-Cola trucks rolled into the parking lot around the same time. An exchange of bottles and cans were made once again. Unbeknownst to Michelle, Caroline had been following Phillip every single morning for the past five weeks. She discovered a pattern with his driving. Only on Wednesdays and Saturdays did he meet Harrison here in the parking lot of Isotopes Park where the two brothers spoke briefly before swapping beverages.

On the other days of the week, Phillip would drive his normal route without this additional stop. He always timed his stops perfectly though so that he arrived at each stop at a specific time. He undoubtedly had gone to some length to time the traffic light patterns while calculating traffic flow. Why this was so important still remained a mystery to Caroline.

"Let's do it, Lucy," Caroline said to her dog. "Let's go on a little trip today." Lucy wagged her tail and barked. Caroline had almost forgotten to let Lucy out of the truck. She quickly let her jump out of the Land Rover. She ran around for a few minutes sniffing and enjoying the spring smells before Caroline called for her to get back into the truck. "Let's go Lucy," she said as the Rio-Cola trucks were pulling out of the lot.

Caroline and Lucy had not been on the highway more than twenty miles when Caroline's phone rang.

"Hi Caroline," her mom said. "Did you hear about Reed?" she asked.

"Hi Mom, and no. What happened?" Caroline asked.

Reed was Rachel's youngest son who always pretended to be the *Six Million Dollar Man* when he was a toddler. He loved baseball from day one and always told everyone that he had a bionic arm. If the truth were told, that was Reed's way of being humble instead of bragging about his powerful pitching arm.

"He broke his arm yesterday," she began to explain.

Carolyn immediately interrupted before her mom even had a chance to explain, "Oh, no. Was it his pitching arm?"

"No, Carolyn. Fortunately, it was his right arm," she said. "He was racing up the stairs in front of his school before the bell rang when he slipped on some ice."

"I thought you said it was in the high forty's a few days ago, mom," Carolyn questioned her mom.

"Well, it was a few days ago. You know how winter weather is around here. There's always a spring snow. We got three inches during the night on Thursday."

"Does Reed need surgery or anything? Caroline questioned.

"I don't think so, but you probably need to talk to Rachel," she said.

"How are you and dad?" Caroline continued to ask.

Caroline usually spoke with her parents at least once a week. She knew about all of their doctor appointments, what food they prepared for their daily meals, and who won the poker game each week. They had been playing cards every Friday night for the last eight or nine years with four other couples. Each week they rotated houses so everyone had a chance to host. It was always small chatter, but it helped Caroline stay rooted with her parents' friends and folks from her hometown. Her mom couldn't go to the grocery store without someone asking about Caroline.

"Oh, we're fine. It's the same ol' stuff happening around here. It snows a little, thaws, and snows some more. Spring will be here soon. I can hear the birds outside my bedroom window now," her mother explained. "How are you doing dear?"

"I'm okay, mom. I'm so busy all the time that I don't have much time to sit around and mope. I'm just trying to move on with life. Work has been steady. On top of that I meet several times a month with the guys at Striking High. Business has actually increased there since I hired the marketing guy from Battle Creek. I really don't do much with it, other than agree with the decisions that are being made. I question the guys occasionally mostly because I don't understand something. It's nice because I get Cal's salary on top of my regular salary."

"We're planning to come down to see your new place once you are completely settled in. We were hoping Rachel and the kids can come too," her mother continued.

Caroline was excited to hear that news. Their last visit was dreadful, and she was hopeful their next trip would be relaxing. "I would love for you to see my new house. It really doesn't matter to me when you come. I still have all of my vacation coming this year. I thought I might come home to Racine for a couple weeks too, mom. Living in a new house definitely helps. Everything in the old house reminded me of Cal. At least I'm not taunted by his memory every time I turn the corner now in my new place. I wish it weren't so quiet all the time, but I'm kind of used to the silence now."

"Well, dad and I will talk to your sister, and let you know what works best for us. I need to make a quick trip to the grocery store to get some bread and butter, so I'll let you go for now. I love you, honey."

"Thanks, mom. I love you too," Caroline said before hanging up.

The ride was going much faster than Caroline imaged without Michelle to keep her company. Her roommate from college called shortly after she spoke with her mom, and then her sister rang. Rachel shared the details of Reed's mishap with Caroline. They talked about a family visit, the kids, the weather, and everything else imaginable. More importantly was the fact that they laughed together again for the first time in months. Rachel had shared a comical story about a customer.

Caroline was relieved that her Land Rover was equipped with hands free service. She would have had a kink in her neck and elbow by now if she had to hold the phone up to her ear. She drove along observing the dry, parched land wondering why some many towns and cities had been established in such arid places out west. About ten minutes north of Las Cruces, Caroline received a fourth call. It was Michelle.

"Hi Caroline. Are we still going biking this afternoon?" Michelle asked.

"Oh Michelle, I completely forgot. I don't think I'll be able to go after all," Caroline replied.

"Why not, Caroline?"

"I'm working."

"You didn't tell me you were going to work today," Caroline snarled.

"I didn't know I would be, Caroline."

At this point Caroline realized her conversation wasn't headed in a positive direction. She knew Michelle well enough to know that she would continue to pry until she heard exactly where Caroline was going and what Caroline was doing. She did not want Caroline to know. She did not like to lie either. She went out of her way to be honest one hundred percent of the time.

"Where are you?" Michelle continued to question.

Caroline did not want to jeopardize her chances of learning more about the whereabouts of her husband. She had a split second to tell the truth or fabricate a story.

"I'm headed to a vendor."

"You're not following Henry, are you?" Michelle continued the questioning as Caroline had predicted. She just didn't expect that question to be asked.

"No, I'm not Michelle."

The words just flowed effortlessly out of Caroline's mouth. She didn't mean to lie, but it just happened. She immediately felt horrible. "What am I doing?" she thought. Caroline then looked ahead and realized that the truck was gone. It was no longer out in front of her. In addition, she had already passed the exit ramp for the mall in Las Cruces. "Phew, I didn't fib after all," she thought trying to reckon with her conscious.

"I've got to go, Michelle. I'll call when I get back," she quickly said has she hung up the phone.

Caroline's heart began to race. She had spent all this time following the truck, but had been distracted so many times with phone calls that she didn't even recognize the truck's exit off the highway. She tried to remember the last mile marker or exit that she actually saw the truck. She couldn't.

"What should I do, Lucy?" she questioned her dog. "I've lost Harrison."

Lucy perked up from her long nap wagging her tail like she did whenever Caroline spoke to her.

"I guess I should get off the highway and turn around. Maybe he stopped at the mall exit like he did last time." she explained to Lucy who was still willing to listen. Fortunately for her, the mall was only a mile down the road. She could take the boulevard that paralleled the highway or she could jump back on the highway. In another split second decision, Caroline decided to get back on the highway. She didn't remember passing Harrison on the highway, but there was always that possibility. He could have been just a few miles behind her. If so, she would be able to see him passing, heading south towards El Paso.

She kept her eyes on the vehicles heading south, but there were no signs of any Rio-Cola truck. She exited the highway a second time and drove towards the mall. She would look for him first before getting gas. As she turned onto South Telshor Boulevard, she could see a truck in the distance. It was parked across the parking lot from Five Guys again. Her moment of panic subsided.

She drove up to the truck close enough to see the flag decal and truck number. It was Harrison's truck. Caroline, felt a sigh of relief. He apparently must like hamburgers a lot to come back to this place again. Caroline turned around and headed back towards the gas station. She would walk Lucy on leash while filling the tank. She didn't want to take any chances of Lucy snatching a second hamburger.

Caroline had just tightened the gas cap when she saw Harrison drive by, heading towards the highway. It didn't take him long at all to get his lunch today. Caroline snatched the receipt that was slowly printing from the pump outside and jumped back into her truck. She and Lucy were on the road again. They followed Harrison down into El Paso just as Caroline had done previously.

Harrison drove through the city and continued down the highway towards San Antonio. Caroline thought for sure that Michelle had said that Harrison had moved to El Paso, not San Antonio. It was still five hundred and thirty-six miles away according to the road sign. Caroline was grateful to see Harrison use a signal as he approached the Fabens, Texas exit ramp, about twenty-five miles from El Paso. She had no idea why he would be stopping here. It was a very small town not too far from the Mexican border. She knew the Southern Pacific Railroad ran through this town, but other than that she had never heard of anything significant about this place.

Caroline slowed way down so Harrison could not see her exit the highway. It would be obvious if she pulled off with him because there wasn't a single car around. He was the lone driver. The barren fields of weed brush and cacti were their only companions. She waited several minutes before she turned off the highway onto route 793, allowing Harrison to drive into town. A small landing strip was down the road about a half-mile from the exit. As Caroline drove by it she could see the Rio-Cola truck in the distance parked in front of a building.

She pulled to the side of the road and carefully took her binoculars out of their protective covering. She watched Harrison unload ten cases of cola and place them on the sidewalk outside of Flicker's Pizza near the backdoor that was adjacent to the tracks. "Why wouldn't he take them inside?" she wondered. It was almost eighty degrees outside now. Once again, this was another thing that didn't jive in her mind. Harrison then walked to the other side of the truck and unloaded five more cases of beverages that he took inside the building. "If the restaurant didn't need those beverages, who did?" Caroline asked Lucy.

Caroline swiftly turned her truck around and headed back towards the highway. She knew she couldn't stay parked there when Harrison drove by or she would surely be noticed. There was no place to hide at the entrance to the highway either. Caroline decided to head back towards El Paso. She would get off at the next exit and hope for the truck to pass so she could follow him back into town. She was completely out of sight by the time Harrison returned.

"Lucy, it's him. It's Harrison," she shouted when she saw the flag on the truck. Placing the binoculars back down on the seat of her truck, she pulled back onto the road and back onto the highway. By now Caroline had learned to hide behind trucks and other traffic rather well. She followed Harrison back to the plant where he pulled the truck inside the loading docks. Five minutes later he was pulling out of the parking lot driving a slate blue Mustang convertible. It wasn't the family car that she expected to see him driving, but with a family of four, she guessed any car was an option. Michelle followed him to a nice residential area about five miles from the plant where he lived. His boys were playing basketball in their driveway when he arrived home. It was only two o'clock in the afternoon.

Carolyn didn't know what to do now. She parked around the block for fifteen minutes trying to device another plan. She drove back to the plant and waited for thirty more minutes. One truck pulled in, and the driver drove away a few minutes later. It basically looked like the plant was closed for the day. Carolyn had acquired a little new information, but nothing substantial.

There was no doubt in her mind that the ten cases of cola probably contained something other than cola. Appearing to look like a soft drink, they made a clever disguise. She assumed someone else would be stopping to retrieve the cases left behind the pizzeria. It was close enough to the railroad tracks, that perhaps even a train might stop for an additional pickup to transport them elsewhere. Without spending countless hours monitoring the pickup in Fabens, Caroline really had no other leads. Even if she did have something else to go on, what does it have to do with her husband? She could not connect the dots or determine if this had anything to do with Cal's disappearance.

"Okay, Lucy, let's find a park for you to run around for a few minutes before heading home," she said. She remembered one of her coworkers telling someone a few months ago that there was a new riverside park downtown. It was easy to locate, so Caroline took Lucy there.

Chapter Eleven
MICHELLE QUINN

Joshua and I had pulled up to Michelle's house about the same time when Jason and his wife, Julie, arrived. The cowboy was already there. My anxiety level was much higher than normal. I had not told the guys anything about my Rio-Cola discovery, and I rarely spoke with Julie. She and Jason had married about a year ago, but she was not a cyclist so we did not see her often.

Michelle was her typical self, dressed perfectly for the occasion and waiting for us at the door.

"Come in guys, come in," Michelle robustly announced.

We all walked through the door into the kitchen, and perched on his saddle at the granite counter was the cowboy himself. He stood as we entered. His boots were polished.

"I want to introduce each of you to Phillip," Michelle said gleaming proud, as she made her introductions.

He shook everyone's hand before approaching me. To my surprise, he bent down and kissed me on the cheek. "Finally," he said. "You are Michelle's amazing friend that I finally have the privilege to meet."

"Thank you, Phillip, I'm happy to meet you too. Michelle has only said wonderful things about you," I replied, hoping he wouldn't feel the quaver of my voice nor the shaking every bone in my body. Like Michelle had warned, he was utterly charming. Although I had a lot of questions that I wanted to ask him, I immediately felt at peace with him. The questions probably would have to wait since I didn't want to share my findings with Josh or Jason.

As Michelle was offering drinks to the others, Phillip looked me straight in the eyes, gently placed his hands on my shoulders, and said, "I'm sorry about Calvin. Michelle told me about that dreaded day and the location where it happened. She probably told you already that my route is in that neighborhood too. I actually drive that street everyday," he continued. "I didn't know anything about it, Caroline. I was in San Bernardino that week visiting my sister and her family. Michelle talks about you all the time, and I couldn't figure out why I could never meet you until now. She finally told me last night that you thought I was the driver of the Rio-Cola truck. I wasn't Caroline."

"You weren't?" I asked. "The police deputy told me that the driver was a regular who had been with the company almost three years. The driver was interviewed along with two other drivers from the other trucks. They were the last people to see my husband," I explained.

"I even showed Michelle my airline ticket stub from the trip when she was over last night. I have photos on Facebook to prove I was with my nieces and nephew too," he said. "Please believe me, Caroline."

"You look a lot like the driver I saw in the video," I explained.

"It couldn't have been me. I wasn't there," he said again.

By now Michelle had walked up to me and placed her arm around my shoulders. "Please believe him, Caroline. He showed me all kinds of proof last night that he was out of town. He even showed me his credit card expenditures. He was in California, Caroline. If you like, I am sure he can show you too," she said. "I wanted you to hear it from him first, rather than me. I hope that was okay."

"That's fine," I said. "If you have proof then there's no need for me to second guess you. Now you just need to live up to the reputation that Michelle has branded on you," I said jokingly.

"I am truly sorry for your loss, Caroline. And, hopefully, you will see for yourself that I am a respectable man."

"From the sounds of it, I think you are a keeper," I said to him smiling.

Michelle then looked at Phillip and asked, "Do you mind putting the steaks on the grill?"

"Well, Jason and Joshua, it looks like you have some fierce competition as grill masters. The cowboy is working the grill tonight," I said. They all chuckled as the guys walked outside to the patio.

"What have you been up to lately, Julie?" I asked as she and I sat at the counter stools nibbling on hors d'oeuvres that were placed along the counter.

"Well," she said as she sipped a glass of water with lemon, "I haven't been feeling too well lately."

Neither Michelle nor I gave her a chance to finish what she was saying. We both yelled at the same time.

"No, you're not."

"Yes," she immediately reciprocated.

I grabbed her right away and hugged her as the guys

came running inside to hear what the commotion was all about.

"Congratulations Jason," I said as he entered the room. I then ran up to him to hug him too.

"I was going to tell you tonight," he said. "It looks like Julie beat me to it."

"It was the lemon water," Michelle said. "She didn't have to say anything."

"Yea, that can be a give away," Jason said.

"Do you know whether you are having a boy or girl yet?" I asked.

"No, since it's our first, we are going to be surprised," Julie said. "It's so easy to decorate a nursery these days, and add finishing touches once the baby is born."

"We'll be happy regardless," Jason added.

"I'm so excited for you both," Michelle told the couple. "Just let Caroline and me know if you would like us to host a baby shower. We'll be thrilled to do that for you."

"Definitely," I added. "We can have it at my place too, if you like."

The guys grabbed their beers and headed back out doors to turn the steaks.

After dinner Michelle served vanilla ice cream topped with fresh peaches and caramel sauce. It was delicious. Since most of the dinner conversation was geared around Jason and Julie, I finally had the chance to ask the one thing about Phillip that I had been dying to know all evening. "Please tell me, cowboy, how did you ever become a Rio-Cola driver?"

"Michelle asked me that same question on our first date," he began. "I really needed a position where I could work morning hours. I didn't have a lot of options, but this was the easiest job to get. My brother, Henry, who lives in El Paso, got the job for me. He works for Rio-Cola down there."

"Why just morning hours?" I continued.

"I'm a college professor at the University of New Mexico. I have taken a sabbatical to work on my doctorate in linguistics. My undergraduate degree was in English."

Joshua and I both looked at each other at the same time with a look of confusion. At that moment, I knew what he was thinking and he knew what I was thinking. I nodded for him to ask the question.

"Phillip, if you are on sabbatical, why do you need to work another job?" he asked. "Don't you get paid for your sabbatical?"

"I do. I am trying to fund a new nonprofit organization that I plan to open once I am finished with my doctorate. My linguistic dissertation is geared around special needs children learning foreign languages as second languages. Currently, they are not typically offered any secondary languages in school. I have discovered through research that some special needs children actually function better using a different language other than English. Their minds are structured differently allowing them to advance to a higher functional level with alternative languages."

I think everyone sitting in the living room was stunned. The attractive and charming Rio Cola delivery driver was an educated man. The cowboy continued his explanation.

"English is a Germanic language, and even though it is used worldwide, it has some complexities that make it difficult for some people. There are many instances where word tenses and phonetics don't make logical sense. In addition, very little inflection is used compared to other languages. For some people this has become a barrier too great to overcome. I am hopeful in time that my nonprofit can develop better testing which will allow those struggling to find an auxiliary language giving them the ability to function more independently. The key is finding the language that best suits their level of brain function."

"Wow," Julie said. "That's impressive."

"I'm not trying to impress anyone. I'm just trying to help children. Most people rely on the fact that everyone is born into a given language that becomes the basis for all of their learning. My discovery is that some children, labeled with learning disabilities, may be perfectly fine if given the chance to navigate with a language more suitable for their learning styles."

"It's still impressive regardless," I said.

"Joshua, to better answer your question. I decided that I needed to work an extra job for four full years to raise enough money to fund the nonprofit. Once it's established, I will be able to continue my research with grant monies. I didn't want to rely on other people's money to fund this project until I knew there was some merit to it. I have nine months to go before I permanently resign as a Rio-Cola delivery driver."

"Well, Michelle, it looks to me like you have chosen a doozy," Jason remarked. "I'm impressed as well."

Phillip then asked Joshua and Jason their line of work. He knew the guys biked with us a lot, but Michelle never told him anything else about them. Joshua explained that he owned the bike store just down the street from the 66 Diner. "It started as a part-time job," Josh began, "fixing bikes, to pay my way through college. One thing led to another and before I knew it, I was opening a store."

Jason was an electrical engineer for Honeywell, one of the larger employers in Albuquerque. He told all of us about his work on the courthouse and renovations to the correctional facility. I couldn't believe the miles of cables needed to wire a building. It was fascinating.

"Well, you might be named the new Grill Master, Phillip," Jason said after taking his first bite of steak. "This is delicious. I'll probably need a replacement in a few shorts months, anyway," he said with a grin.

"Oh, it sounds to me like you and Joshua have it down to a science. I wouldn't want to mess up your rhythm," Phillip commented back.

After dinner, we played bocce ball. Michelle challenged the men to a 'gals versus guys' game. I wasn't too sure that the ladies would come out on top, but Michelle was always up for a challenge. It came down to a tiebreaker, and Michelle didn't let us down. She had the last throw of the evening. Phillip had already thrown his ball within a foot of the white ball. Michelle needed to either knock his ball away or get closer than a foot.

"Decisions, decisions, uh, Michelle," I teased. "You either need to come out the hero and or let your new beau pretend to be one," I joked.

"Phillip doesn't have a chance," she responded back with complete confidence. She then took a deep breath and rolled the ball across the lawn. To all of our surprise, she hit

Phillip's ball on the left forcing it to roll a few inches to the right, while her ball rolled next to the white ball. She did it.

All the ladies cheered while the men proclaimed that it was pure luck. Phillip, however, went up to his new girlfriend, and said, "Congratulations, Michelle, you got me beat this time, but I'll get the next one." He then kissed her.

Jason and Julie were the first to leave around ten, followed shortly afterwards by Joshua. I stayed longer to help Michelle and Phillip clean up. I also wanted to be alone with them for a few minutes too. "Phillip," I asked, "Does Rio Cola ever do tours of their facility?"

"I'm not one hundred percent sure, but I think we do. I'm rarely in the building, just long enough to load my truck, but I remember one of the drivers sticking around because his daughter was coming with her class from school."

"I've never been on a tour myself, but I think it would make an interesting one. Quinn, I'm willing to chaperone your class if you decide to take one" I said. I didn't want to give Michelle a chance to say 'no' because I really wanted to get inside the building. Although, Phillip appeared to be charming, I still had some doubts.

"Oh, that's a great idea, Caroline. What do you think Quinn? Huh, Quinn?" he said jokingly as he leaned over Michelle's shoulders pulling her into his body as he poked her in the sides trying to get her to laugh. Then he looked at me and said, "Michelle told me about her name. You don't have to call her Quinn anymore when I'm around. I'm getting used to her first name, but I do like her middle name so it might stick with me."

I chuckled. "I was wondering why you were calling her Michelle earlier," I commented back, looking a Michelle with a look of inquiry.

"I knew I would have to do some explaining with everyone coming over tonight, and I really didn't want to explain details to the guys. They would mock and tease me for weeks to come. I either had to come clean with Phillip about my name or tell the guys I had met him in the grocery store. I figured it would be easier telling Phillip, and I would get less teasing from the guys," she said now giggling.

"Anyway, Michelle," Phillip said kissing her on the cheek, "do you want me to set up a tour for your class?" he asked.

She then turned around to face Phillip who was still holding her from behind and said, "I think my students would have a blast going through the facility. Anytime will work for me. I just need a week's notice to get enough drivers for carpooling."

"Okay. Plan on me, Michelle," I said as I headed towards the door. "It was nice meeting you Phillip. You take good care of my friend. I'll see you guys later."

"It was a pleasure meeting you too, Caroline. Good night.

Chapter Twelve

ON THE ROAD AGAIN

"Caroline, wake up. Caroline, wake up," I heard a familiar voice call out.

I thought I was dreaming as I turned over to see Lucy run up to where the utterance was coming outside the French doors of my bedroom that overlooked the pool. In all the nights that I had lived in my new home, never once had I pulled the window treatments closed, until last night. On many sleepless nights, I would gaze into the stars or watch the reflection of the moon ripple across the water of the pool wondering if my husband could see the same night sky. Last night I decided to block the early morning sun. I was exhausted. I no longer had a Rio Cola truck to chase, but now only a theory that would be very difficult to prove. I thought I would try to catch up on missed sleep.

Lucy's tail was swaying back and forth as she stuck her head behind the drapery that was pulled closed. Not once did she bark, a sure sign that my intruder was someone she liked. I could see the front wheel of a bike and the tips of a biking shoe when Lucy nudged her head through the opening. "What do you want Michelle?" I mumbled through my sheets. Only Michelle would ride over to my house.

"Let me in," she said.

I crawled out of bed, pulled back the curtain, and opened

the door. "What's wrong with the front door?" I asked as she stepped foot into my room.

"I tried, but no one answered," she said again.

Michelle then proceeded to take off her biking gloves and project her left hand forward towards me. "No way," I said as she jumped up and down with excitement. I hugged her tight for a moment. "Tell me all about it," I said as I crawled back under my covers, still half asleep.

Michelle did not appreciate the darkness of my room on this beautiful Saturday morning. Before jumping onto my bed, she pulled the drapes open entirely, allowing the light to illuminate the room. She then began waiving her hand, generating scattered rainbows all over the walls from the reflection of her newly acquired diamond marquise. I covered my eyes- the brightness was too intense for me.

"So much for a little extra sleep," I muttered. Michelle didn't even give me a chance to fall back asleep.

"It happened last night," she began. "Phillip asked if I would like to go on a picnic last night. He picked me up around six. We drove up to Mosca Peak to watch the sunset. We hiked up the trails a little ways where we found the perfect spot for our picnic. He had packed a basket with fresh southwest chicken sandwiches on crescent rolls, fresh vegetables and dip, and cheese and crackers. He laid a lawn blanket on the ground before setting up with his fine china."

"Really, a lawn blanket and fine china?" I asked. "The hundreds of times we have eaten brown bag lunches in the mountains while we were riding, and you get a lawn blanket and china for the first time ever?"

"Yea, wasn't that nice," Michelle said with a grin as wide as any canyon. "He then pulled out a chilled bottle of champagne with glass wine goblets. It was so incredibly romantic. After we ate, he told me to wait a few minutes while he went down to his car to get his guitar."

"He plays the guitar?" I asked, now fully out from beneath my covers.

"Yes, he does and the piano too," Michelle informed me.

"Dang, this guy is too perfect," I said.

"It gets even better, Caroline. After he played several songs, and we cuddled and kissed, and watched the sun begin to set, he then got down on one knee and began playing another song, a song that he had written. I was in such shock the first time I heard it, that I asked him to play it again. The song was his proposal.

"He asked you to marry him in a song?" I shouted. "That is the coolest thing ever. He wrote a song for you? Oh, Michelle, you are just a special lady. What did you say to him after he was done singing?"

"I kissed him and said, 'yes.' He then reached into his guitar case and pulled out this ring and placed it on my finger. I just melted in his arms again."

"That is so cool," I said again as I propped myself up against my pillow. "He's one heck of a cowboy."

"Hey, it's Saturday and he's working this morning, so let's go for a ride," Michelle said. "It's another beautiful morning."

Michelle was right. We should go for a ride together. It had been a long time since we had cycled together.

"Where do you want to go?" I asked.

"Let's ride the trails by Piedra Lisa Park, then I can take you past Phillip's house," Michelle suggested.

"Oh, where does he live?" I asked.

"Juan Taboo Hills."

"He lives that close to us?" I questioned, puzzled that he lived on this side of town. I assumed that he lived closer to the university near my old house.

"He lives in the home that he grew up in," Michelle explained. "His dad passed away seven years ago. His mom lived alone for almost five years, but then asked him to move back home to help out with lawn work and home maintenance. To help save money for his venture, he moved back home when he took the delivery position. He also told me that he really missed not having a piano to play every day. His mom has a baby grand. They live near the dam."

"Wow," I said. "He just seems like a loving, caring guy. Hey, do you want to pack lunches while I get dressed and take care of Lucy? The usual works for me."

Michelle went into the kitchen to pack our lunches. We typically ate the same thing almost every time we rode; peanut butter and jelly sandwiches, kettle chips, carrots, and cookies. We would need the protein from the peanut butter, and the salt from the chips to help maintain our energy level. Before leaving, we checked our tires to make sure the air pressure was just right and grabbed two frozen water bottles out of the freezer.

"Let me draft behind you," I told Michelle as I placed my shoe into the toe clip. There was a slight breeze causing a head wind on our trip out. Since Michelle was the stronger rider, I needed any extra help I could find to keep up with her pace.

Normally, we would take our trail bikes out, but today we were taking our road bikes since much of our ride would be on pavement rather than trails. There was only one small stretch that was unpaved, and it was a heavily traveled cinder trail making the ground packed firm.

I fastened the strap of my helmet and put on my sunglasses as we headed down the road passed the young Arabian fillies. "Slow down until I get my legs loosened up," I told Michelle from behind. I was trailing about a foot from her back wheel. It felt good to be on my road bike again. I had gone on several mountain runs over the last two months, but this was the first time I took my road bike out since Cal's disappearance. When I lived in the city, I took my bike everywhere. The breeze felt nice. It was warm, but not too hot yet.

"Road kill right," Michelle yelled as she pointed down to the ground with her right hand forewarning me of the hazard in the road ahead. We both looked in our rearview mirrors to confirm no cars were passing us at that moment. Mine was attached to my handlebars, but Michelle wore a small one off the side of her helmet, not too far from her left temple. We both swerved at the same time to avoid the desert tortoise. It was uncommon for us to see those on the road, but this morning we did. In the city, we often would see squirrels. On our way out to the mountains, long-tailed weasels, skunks, and snakes were the most common type of road kill that we saw.

Years ago, after I first moved to New Mexico, when I had just joined the cycling club, I was coming back down out of the mountains before sunset. The roads were wet from a mountain rain. I was riding with three other cyclists including Michelle.

"Do you remember that day when we saw the armadillo?" I asked Michelle. "I was just thinking about that when you yelled 'road kill.'"

"Yea, I thought you were going to kill us all," Michelle yelled loud enough so I could hear her speak.

"I still laugh about that today," I said.

"It wouldn't have been funny, if we had all crashed and burned," she reminded me.

We were riding along, and out of nowhere, an armadillo jumped about six feet into the air right before scrambling across the road. Apparently, we scared the living daylights out of it, because it took off across the road like there was no tomorrow. I thought it scared the living day lights out of me. I was the second biker in the pack, and I slammed my brakes on without telling Michelle or Jason who were riding behind me. I just about caused the biggest crash ever. Being experienced cyclists, they both were able to swerve around me just in the nick of time. We stopped and regrouped, and I got a lecture from everyone that I rightly deserved. It was the craziest looking thing I had ever seen. It came out of nowhere and I thought it was going to land on my face.

I certainly learned a lesson that day. When you are riding in a pack with other cyclists, you must talk and let them know exactly what you are doing. If you are going to brake, you need to shout, 'braking.' If you plan to swerve away from something in the street, you need to yell, 'pothole,' road kill,' 'car door,' or whatever it is that's in the way. I had never been a part of a cycling group before so I had no clue that there were rules to biking.

It took Michelle and me about fifty minutes to ride the ten miles to the opening of the park trail. I didn't realize how sore I would be. My shoulders were stinging from the bending over onto my handlebars and my buttocks were aching from the narrower saddle on my road bike. I didn't care. I was doing the one thing that I loved to do with my best friend. The worries of the Terric brothers and my lost husband were temporarily gone.

The trail was quiet when we arrived. We took it about five more miles before it ended into the cinder trail. At that point, we dismounted from our bikes and hid them behind some trees while we found a place to eat our lunch. We hiked up the mountain a little ways to a clearing where a waterfall gushed down into a ravine. During the spring and early summer months, water gushed easily down the mountains. During the late summer and fall, the roar would drown into an oasis past the trail.

I looked over at Michelle as she took off her helmet. Her blond hair, wet from sweat, was pasted to her head while perspiration from the heat of the day poured down her face. Her long ponytail swagged against her back. I couldn't have looked any better, but it didn't matter. We were exhilarated from our fifteen-mile ride. The pain that we had encountered was momentarily gone. Our muscles felt alive. It was an anomalous feeling.

"Awe, this is refreshing," Michelle said as she bent over to wash her face in the cold stream.

One by one I took off my helmet, gloves, shoes and socks, and carefully stepped foot into the freezing water. It was cold, but completely refreshing. I had forgotten the sensation of spring water so cold that it was almost numbing. We both made our way to a large boulder about twenty feet round in the middle of the river down stream from the waterfall where we sat down to eat our lunch. The stone was cool, and water splashed onto one side of it leaving sprays and droplets on the rock.

Our peanut butter and jelly sandwiches tasted as good as any steak dinner. Our bodies needed energy for the second half of our journey. It would be about a thirty-two mile ride for me today, but that wasn't of any concern. I dangled my feet in the water a few more minutes after eating my lunch before I took them out and laid-back against the rock. I closed my eyes as I waited for my legs to dry. I could feel the warm sun beat down on my eyes as I rested silently with them closed. The birds were singing while the water continued to rumble upstream as it fell to the bottom of the canyon. I was relaxed.

"Caroline, wake up. Caroline, wake up," I heard a familiar voice call out for the second time today as Michelle reached over to touch my arm.

I must have fallen asleep.

Oblivious to the question Michelle had just asked, she said "Didn't you hear me?"

"Um, no, I guess I didn't," I told her.

I was just talking about wedding plans, and I asked if we could have the wedding at your house," she said again.

"What?" I said surprised as I rolled over on my elbow to propped myself up. "Don't you want to get married in a church?"

"No. I don't think I do," Michelle answered back. "I don't think we could even find a place now if we tried," she

142

continued to say.

"What do you mean?" I asked.

"Well, we want to get married right away. There won't be any reception halls or churches even available this time of year. You're back yard will be perfect. We want it to be small and simple, maybe around fifty guests."

"How soon is soon?"

"The last Saturday in May, the day after school gets out."

"Michelle, you haven't even known this guy for more than ten weeks," I responded.

"I know, Caroline, but that's not going to change how we feel about each other. It's not like we are twenty-two. We are both in our thirties and know what we want in a spouse," she explained. "Besides, you knew that you wanted to marry Cal after your third date, and you were only twenty-one at the time."

"Yea, but I didn't marry him two months later," I rebutted. "Have you even met his brother yet? You know, the guy who is still one of my suspects."

"No, I haven't met him yet, but he's planning to come this weekend. I just don't think Phillip or Henry had anything to do with Cal's disappearance," Michelle refuted. "You know, Caroline, there isn't anything in the world that I want more for you than to have Calvin back. I feel helpless though. I've helped you in every way possible. I don't know what else I can do to help. If there's anything else you want from me, please ask. I can't stop living because of what happened to Calvin. I don't want you to stop living either. Isn't that why you moved, and why we had the big party…. to help you move on with your life? I know how hard this must be for you, but I truly love the guy. I know, we've only been dating two and a half months. But, Caroline, these last couple of months have been the best months of my life. Can't you see how happy I am?"

"I know, Michelle. I can see it all over your face. You are so different now than you were before you met Phillip. He brings the best out of you. And, I want you to be happy. There's no hiding the fact that you are in love. I just can't stop thinking about 053171. You know, Harrison's truck with the Mexican flag."

Michelle always tried to look at the positive side of things. "Is it possible that there are two trucks with the same number?" she asked cautiously, not to offend me.

"We both know that all things are possible," I acknowledged. "But, you have to admit that the circumstances are still unsettling."

"Caroline, we have talked about this before. You know that I agree with you. I just think that you would see things differently if you got to know Phillip the way I know him."

"Maybe. But, how can I trust anyone anymore... except you, of course? I don't think I have a choice, but to act cautiously. Don't you have any concerns at all about marrying him too soon?" Without giving Michelle a chance to answer, I continued. "I do. There is still something suspicious about the two brothers exchanging coke. What happens if he's not the perfect man he appears to be?" I then asked.

"Well, no one is perfect, so I guess he'll fit in with the rest of the crowd," Michelle joked. It didn't matter where we were, if a joke could be found, Michelle was the person to find it. "I've been seeing him for ten weeks now, Caroline, and it's been the best ten weeks of my life. Our relationship is so much better than the one I had with Alex. I can't believe now, that I was actually going to marry Alex."

"What do you think of his mom?" I then asked. "Does she like you? Do you like her?"

"We get along beautifully. She is the dearest woman I've ever met. She took me out for lunch a couple weekends ago, just one on one time. She said she wanted to get to know me as a person without Phillip around. We talked about his childhood, my childhood, the church he attended, our families, our careers, and all kinds of stuff."

"Did she say anything at all about him or his brother that would help me find Calvin?"

"No. She told me how she met Phillip's dad. He was a young pilot when they first met. He had a layover in San Francisco where she was vacationing with her family. She met him in the hotel where they were both staying. When they learned they were both from Albuquerque, they exchanged phone numbers. Since he traveled a lot, they dated for almost two years, she said, before they got married."

"Did she say anything else?" I asked.

"No, not really. She reminded me that the key to any marriage is forgiveness. They had been married almost thirty years."

"Why would she tell you that?"

"I don't know. She said that she almost didn't marry him because she had a fling when they first started dating. She asked him for a second chance so he gave it to her. She's a wonderful woman, Caroline. I think you will like her. So, Caroline, can we have the wedding at your house or do you plan to hold a grudge forever?"

"Are you completely sure, without any doubts at all, that this is the right man for you?" I then asked.

Michelle didn't hesitate at all, "I don't think anyone can be more certain than I am right now. I know for sure that he is the right husband for me."

My questions continued. "What happens in two months or in two years, if I discover that he was involved in the disappearance of Cal?"

I knew that Caroline didn't want to hear me talk this way, but I needed to express my concerns. I didn't want it on my conscious if anything were to happen. Her parents weren't going to talk to her about this. They didn't know all the details. All of our friends thought they were the perfect pair. I wasn't willing to lose another friend either. I had already lost Cal. I couldn't handle Michelle walking out of my life if I didn't support her, even if her decision was in haste.

"I don't believe that will ever happen, but if it does, then you and I will both know that I made a huge mistake. I will have to deal with the consequences."

"Do your parents like him?" I asked as the water continued to gush all around us swirling down the mountainside towards the valley below.

"Of course they do," Michelle answered. "Who doesn't like Phillip?"

She did have a good point. Everybody loved Phillip. Michelle's family liked him and so did all of our friends.

"So, is there any possibility, you will let me have our wedding at your place?" Michelle asked again.

"I hope I'm wrong, Michelle. I do like him, you know. If the events were different, this wouldn't even be a concern. I promise I won't ever bring this up with you again. My family is coming for Spring Break, so the last weekend in May should be fine," I told her.

"Oh, thank you so much, Caroline," Michelle said as she leaned over to hug me. "I know I'm making the right decision. Will you also be my matron of honor?" she then asked.

"Of course, I will be, Michelle."

"I want the wedding to be very simple. We can have the reception catered too so you can enjoy the day," she said.

Within a few minutes, we were both on our bikes again headed down the trail. What a whirlwind of a day this has been. Only three hours earlier, Michelle showed up unexpectedly at my house to tell me that she was engaged. I decide to go on a bike ride with her, and I am now hosting a wedding and reception.

I continued to ride in Michelle's draft, much further back now though, as we cut around corners and turns through the foot hills as we made our way down out of the mountain towards Phillip's house. We were both slouched over our handle bars with our heads tucked low so we could have the least resistance possible which would give us more speed. We kept our feet parallel to the road unless we were turning a corner when we rotated our pedals a quarter turn to make them perpendicular to the road. If we were going around a bend that turned left, then our right foot would be down closest to the ground while our left leg would be bent at the knee to allow more clearance for the pedal to prevent it from hitting the ground.

This was the moment, coming down out of the mountains, that we became one with our bikes. Our bodies and the motor-less frame on which we sat, leaned together jointly far into the turns, motionless as we defied any road signs suggesting that we ride slower around the bends. Both adrenaline and undaunted bravery kicked in, masquerading any fear of crashing or leaving our tissue embedded on the road surface. One slight jerk of the handle bar or loose gravel could slide the narrow wheels right out from beneath us or any rider, shattering the fragile physique of even the most trained cyclists.

Within minutes, we were out of the mountains and cycling through the streets of Juan Taboo Hills. Riding down hill with a tail wind cut our time in half. The homes in this neighborhood were upscale and well maintained. When we arrived at Phillip's house, we were surprised to see that he was already home. Michelle briefed him on our morning ride through the trails at Piedra Lisa Park as Phillip kindly offered us ice cold water.

"Congratulations," I said after I guzzled down half of my water. "I hear you are quite the romantic."

Phillip laughed. "Is that what Michelle said?" he inquired.

"Anyone who can write and sing a song for his fiancée is a romantic," I claimed. "How about a repeat so I can hear it too?" I asked, not imagining he would ever agree to sing.

"I'll be happy too," he said as he walked into the next room to sit at the antique baby grand piano. It was a beautiful

148

piano with sleek, tapered legs that met the floor with a keystone design. The ivory keys, not common with most pianos found today, had a lustrous sheen.

I was completely shocked again. I never expected the piano to be a part of his repertoire. When Michelle told me about it this morning, I envisioned the cowboy strumming away on his guitar with the sun drowning into the horizon. The maverick was elegant and accomplished too.

"I think I would rather play it on the piano this time around," he said as he gave his fiancée a kiss. "She's not heard it on the piano yet, and it is a little different than the guitar." Michelle sat down beside him, while I sat in a lounge chair directly across from the piano.

There in front of me sat the cowboy, dressed in blue jeans and a tight t-shirt, gazing into the eyes of my best friend. My mouth literally fell open when he began to sing.

I see myself in your eyes, my soul becomes alive
When I touch your skin, a burning yields,
the flames will never die
My heart explodes, the beat moves on, faster than overdrive
I hear your voice; it's magical, the heavens open in the sky

Please stay with me, babe, forever and always
I don't know if I can ever survive again
without you in my life
Hold me tight, love me right, never to deprive
Our love can last a lifetime

I didn't see you coming, that day not so long ago
Your eloquence, your beauty, too much to withhold
Hold my hand, stay with me, now and forevermore
Please say 'I do,' I want you too

I see myself in your eyes, my soul becomes alive
When I touch your skin, a burning yields,
the flames will never die
My heart explodes, the beat moves on, faster than overdrive
I hear your voice; it's magical, the heavens open in the sky

The way you walk, the way you talk,
makes me drop to my knees
In a troubled world we live, your bright smile sets me free
Please come with me, let's sail the seven seas
Please say 'I do,' I want you too

I'm here for you, let my strength comfort you,
let me be the one
Riding high across the plains, forever and always
Let's embrace it, we can make it through
Please say 'I do,' I want you too

I see myself in your eyes, my soul becomes alive
When I touch your skin, a burning yields,
the flames will never die
My heart explodes, the beat moves on, faster than overdrive
I hear your voice; it's magical, the heavens open in the sky

Please stay with me, babe, forever and always
I don't know if I can ever survive again
without you in my life
Hold me tight, love me right, never to deprive
Our love can last a lifetime

I didn't see you coming, that day not so long ago
Your eloquence, your beauty, too much to withhold
Hold my hand, stay with me, now and forevermore
Please say 'I do,' I want you too

Please, honey, say 'I do,' I want you too
Please say 'I do,' I love you

"That is…" I was speechless. Again, I tried to talk. "That is…" I was so overcome with emotions that it took me a moment to speak. "That is the most beautiful song I have ever heard, Phillip. And, Michelle, when you told me how he wrote and sang this beautiful song for you, you failed to mention that he has an incredible voice."

"Thank you, Caroline. It was easy to write because Michelle is such an incredible woman." Phillip then kissed Michelle a second time, despite the sweat still rolling off her cheeks from the ride.

"That was beautiful," Phillip's mom said. She had walked in quietly behind me. I never heard her come into the room.

"Evelyn, I would like you to meet my best friend, Caroline" Michelle said as she introduced me to Phillip's mother.

"Good afternoon, Evelyn. It's nice to meet you," I said. "I don't typically look like this, but Michelle and I just got back from a long bike ride.

"No worries, my dear," Evelyn spoke graciously. "I'm sure I'll see you again soon when the time is more suitable for visiting."

"Well, I need to go home now. I'll see you two later. Tuesday, right?"

"Yep, Tuesday at eleven a.m. at school," Michelle remarked.

"Congratulations again, Michelle and Phillip. It was nice meeting you, Evelyn."

Chapter Thirteen
AN ORDINARY DRINK

The Rio-Cola Bottling Company was intriguing and captivating. Every one of Michelle's students was engaged with the tour from the moment we arrived until the time we left. The kids even asked some interesting questions that most adults would not have considered. I was as impressed with her students as I was the factory.

The facility itself was much larger on the inside than it appeared on the outside. Our first stop was the film room. Once seated and lights dimmed, a nine minute documentary depicted the history of Rio-Cola, a fountain drink, which originated in 1886 in Atlanta, Georgia. It took a full century before the introduction of caffeine free and cherry colas onto the market. A museum, much like the original one in Georgia, housed decades of paraphernalia. I loved the earlier illustrated advertisements of Santa Claus drinking a Cola. I was also most intrigued with the design of the bottle. Beneath bulletproof glass, decades of bottles were displayed portraying the changes over the years.

After the film, we were escorted into the plant itself for the next stage of the tour. I expected to see enormous drums filled with Cola and other cola products being stirred by mammoth metal mixing arms. To my surprise, we saw metal machines with clear plastic tubing projecting down into the bottles themselves. All of the ingredients were blown separately into the bottles, starting first with water then the syrup. Miles of conveyer belts guided glass bottles from place to place.

First, the bottles marched through a sterilization center where they were prepped for the liquid. Once the bottles were dried, hundreds of them were filled simultaneously with each soft drink ingredient before moving on to a scale where each bottle was individually weighed to make sure the proper amount of liquid poured correctly into the bottles. If a bottle was chipped, not filled to the brim, or had the wrong label, it was individually removed from the inventory by workers monitoring the conveyor. Carbonation was the final addition to each drink prior to the bottles being sealed with a cap.

Another part of the plant accommodated similar equipment needed to fill cans and plastic bottles. Each conveyer system was designed specifically to meet the needs of each container. The sealing process used for glass bottles was very different from the cans and plastic bottles. The finished product was either crated or boxed before being delivered to a holding area where it was sorted for deliveries. Although the shelf life was six to nine months long, the company did not like to hold a lot of finished inventory. It wanted to ship fresh product out to consumers as quickly as possible.

After seeing the plant itself, we were allowed to walk by the lab where dozens of people, wearing red lab coats, worked. These were the men and women who continually tried to invent new drinks for consumers. Cameras were not allowed so I could not photograph my findings, but I noticed ten cases of cola sitting by the back door of the lab. In addition, each technician had a miniature scale drum and mixer where they could actually produce, bottle, and seal their own beverages.

The tour ended in a tasting room where every student was able to sample three beverages of choice. Michelle and her students loved the tour. It was the best field trip that I had ever taken.

Later that evening when Michelle and I talked about the field trip, it became unmistakably clear to me that Michelle felt the evidence wasn't compelling enough to make any accusations against Harrison. After seeing the plant, I was rather confident myself that Phillip was innocent of any wrongdoing. He wasn't any part of the production process. He simply arrived early enough each morning to load his truck and make his deliveries. However, there were several things that I still could not explain. My husband was still missing. Phillip exchanged ten cases of cola with Harrison twice a week, and Harrison in return delivered those beverages to a location next to the railroad tracks. In addition, Harrison had complete authority of his facility.

I now needed to make a decision. Should I remain silent or open my mouth? Michelle had just told me two days earlier that she would be meeting Harrison this weekend, specifically Friday evening. That means he would have one delivery, Wednesday morning, prior to meeting Michelle. I could let Michelle marry Phillip without any further questioning, knowing that there were some peculiar behaviors still taking place. I'm not sure a decision to remain silent would be in the best interest of Michelle or me. I had promised her that I would not bring it up again with her. I had every intention of keeping that promise. My only alternative was to approach the men myself.

As I sat in bed deliberating the quandary, I tried to think of every possibility. I took a deep breath as I leaned my head against my cherry headboard and ran my fingers through my hair. I then closed my eyes and asked the question over again to myself, "Should I remain silent or open my mouth?" What will Harrison think when he meets the dog sitter whose dog snatched his hamburger? Will he trust Michelle? What if this was some part of a bigger scheme? The questions tormented me.

When I finally slid under my covers for the night, I tossed and turned. My heart was heavy. I didn't want Michelle to get hurt a second time. My eyelids kept closing, but I couldn't sleep. I had to make a decision.

"Lucy," I said, "I need to confront the brothers tomorrow."

My hands were sweating as I pulled into the parking lot and parked in front of the Rio Cola trucks as the brothers were unloading their ten cases of coke. I knew Phillip would be dumbstruck to see me. I didn't know if this would be my last day on earth or the beginning of a new alliance. And, even if the Terric brothers didn't kill me, Michelle just might. My intuition was talking and I needed to listen.

"Hello Phillip," I began.

"Caroline, what are you doing here?" he responded back in a less than amiable tone.

"Hello Henry."

"Who is this?" Henry asked his brother.

"Henry, this is Caroline, Michelle's best friend. Apparently, Caroline, you already know this is my brother, Henry."

"I need to talk to both of you," I began still shaking in fear of the unknown.

"We are on a time schedule," Henry protested.

"Yes, I know you are. That's why I am interrupting your schedule right now," I responded back.

"We can explain, Caroline, but not right now. Can you let us go, please?" Phillip asked. "I promise we can explain later. I already know this isn't going to be a two minute conversation, is it?"

My plan was already backfiring on me. When I finally found the nerve to confront the issue head on, I got chewed away. Maybe I should have followed Phillip on his entire route. I never followed him for an entire day.

"When do you suggest we meet again?" I asked.

"How about Friday night when Henry is back in town?" Phillip recommended.

I gave in to their demand. "Okay. My place without Michelle though," I said. "And, promise me that you won't say anything to Michelle about this until after we talk?" I added.

"Deal," Phillip said as he and his brother continued to exchange their product.

I got back into my truck and drove off.

"What was that all about Phillip?" Henry asked after I was gone.

"Do you remember hearing about the man who went missing about six months ago from the street corner by the 66 Diner?" Phillip asked.

"No, I don't recall," Henry answered.

"Well, he was the husband of Michelle's best friend, Caroline, whom you just met. She thought I had something to do with it according to what the police told her. But, I was out of town. That was the week we were all in San Bernardino."

I headed straight to work, arriving a few minutes earlier than normal. Friday could not get here soon enough. The next three days, I stayed late at work to avoid any confrontation with Michelle. I even stayed late on Friday so I wouldn't have to think about my upcoming conversation. Michelle must have told Phillip where I lived because they never asked for my address nor did I ever give it to them. They arrived together, shortly after six.

Phillip was much more cordial tonight than he had been on Wednesday morning. "Hi Caroline," he said when Lucy and I greeted him at the door.

"This dog looks familiar," Henry said as Lucy sniffed him up one leg and down the other.

"Come on in. Can I get you a drink?" I asked. "Pepsi? Beer? Water?"

"Water will be fine," they both said politely.

I took them to the living room rather than the back. Earlier in the week, Michelle had asked if she could bring them here at seven thirty to show Phillip and his brother where she planned to hold the wedding and reception. I decided I would show them the outdoors later, when they came back the second time.

I began by sharing the details of Calvin's disappearance with Henry in case Phillip had not explained it to him. I wanted to make sure they both knew exactly why I was targeting them as suspects. I showed them my pictures and explained the differences in the trucks. They were both shocked to hear that I had been following them, and that I knew exactly what time they met, where they go afterwards, and the timing of Phillip's stops prior to arriving at Isotopes Park. I clarified that the time of Cal's disappearance was different than their normal route time by a few minutes, and this was important because Phillip never deviated from his schedule.

I also explained that neither Michelle nor I had any idea who either of them were, let alone the fact that they were broth-ers, when I first asked her to join me in my search. I was going on a hunch when I realized the truck in my photo had a Mexi-can flag while Phillip's truck did not. I must have spoken for a half hour before I even gave the men a chance to respond.

"Wow," Phillip said when I was done saying my peace. "First, I can understand why you thought we might be involved in your husband's disappearance after hearing your full expla-nation. Let us try to fill in some of the unknowns for you the best we can."

"Okay," I said.

"As you and Michelle already know, I was in San Ber-nardino visiting our sister. What I never told either of you is that Henry was there too. We were there for a family reunion. At the time, I didn't know that Henry was even a part of your suspicions," Phillip began.

"I can prove that too," Henry said. "What I can't explain is who was driving my truck. Let me see that picture again."

I showed both brothers the picture once more. They agreed that the man looked similar to both of them, although neither could identify him.

"And, the officer told you that the man they interviewed had been driving this route for three years?" Henry inquired.

"Yes, that's exactly what he told me. He did not give me any names of the drivers though. He claims that he interviewed all three drivers from all three companies."

Henry then gave an explanation of Rio Cola's policy. "Each facility uses substitute drivers when drivers can not make their scheduled routes. These drivers are screened and trained through a temp service that facilitates the schedules. Pepsi, Crystal Springs, Faygo, Jones Soda, Rio-Cola, and Coke all use the same temp service. It saves the company thousands and thousands of dollars yearly since they do not have to provide training or benefits to these drivers. When an employee goes on vacation or calls in sick, the route information is downloaded through a computer program directly to this temp service. We do not have any control over the selection of drivers. I know for sure that this is not one of my regular drivers from El Paso, and I don't believe he's a regular here in Albuquerque. I worked here for many years and never hired the man in your photo. He might be new, but I have never seen him before."

"I haven't either," Phillip answered. "I honestly don't know all of the drivers though."

"I could try to locate this driver, but it has been so many months ago that I doubt I could even get the records from the temp service," Henry stated. "The truck that Phillip drives is the truck that I drove for many years when I first started working for Rio Cola. When I transferred down to El Paso, I decided to keep the same number since it was imbedded into my memory. Since I am the manager, I typically don't drive a truck. This is one of the spare trucks that we keep on site in the event a truck repair can't be made quickly by our mechanics. The employees think I have a special route where I deliver to high profile companies."

"All of our trucks," Henry continued, "include a Mexican decal because we cross the border on a daily basis with many of our trucks. That is one of the identifying symbols that the border control uses to recognize trucks from our plant. How someone got my truck on the day Calvin's disappeared is mind boggling to me. As you know, it's a four-hour trip between the two cities. The driver would have had to come the night before or leave by four in the morning. Someone went out of their way to make it appear as if Phillip or I were driving."

"That photo certainly looks like the man could be our brother," Phillip responded.

I was still puzzled. "Wouldn't you, Henry, need to leave at four in the morning as well?"

"Sometimes, but I often drive up every Tuesday evening and Friday evening?" he explained. "It's a chance for me to visit our mother."

"You are away from your family twice a week?"

"Most weeks, I am," Henry acknowledged. "There have been a few times when Phillip came to El Paso, but not many. It hasn't been easy, but the cash reward has been worth it."

"Cash reward?" I asked.

"Let me explain, Caroline. I am not even authorized to tell you this, but due to your findings and the fact that my brother plans to marry your best friend, I think the secret will be safe with you. Under no circumstances can you ever share this information with anyone," Henry began. "Phillip doesn't even know all the details."

Phillip looked at me with a surprise look on his face. "I don't?" he questioned his brother.

"When I was working here in Albuquerque," Henry began, "one of our chemists discovered an alternative ingredient that he added to the cola. It takes years of testing before any new product ever reaches the public. Like many of the chemists, when they create a new drink, they often take it home to their family members and test it for long periods of time. This man did that very thing. His daughter happened to have an illness that required a high cost drug here in the states. This employee discovered that his daughter became well after drinking the cola for many months. His daughter had been so tired of taking medicine that she stopped taking the drugs without his knowledge. It was by complete accident that they could pin point a correlation between her health and the new drink."

"What is the illness?" I inquired.

"I don't want to say any more or disclose her identity," Harrison responded.

"Every time the chemist tried to get a patent on the product, it was denied. Pharmaceutical companies here in the states are not keen on ideas that interfere with their drugs. The Mexican government is very interested in the product. They are paying Rio Cola a lot of money to provide the drink on a trial basis. That is why I drive up here two days a week to exchange ten cases of Mexican coke for ten cases of this special coke. The Mexican government is giving it to some children who have the same medical needs as the chemist's daughter. The trial will end at the end of Phillip's employment."

"You didn't know about this?" I turned to look at Phillip.

"I thought we were being paid extra money to exchange the cases because the chemist had a new formula that the Mexican official liked better than both Mexican Cola and American Cola," Phillip replied. "I knew it wasn't being distributed yet, but I didn't think much of it."

"So, why do you drop the ten cases off at the back door of the pizzeria?" I asked.

"It's a disguise. If you noticed, I did take pop inside the restaurant as well. A train stops there and picks up the soda at a precise time every Wednesday and Saturday. Everyone thinks that is just the location where the conductor stocks up on Rio Cola. The truth is the cases are being transferred further down the tracks where they are picked up by the Mexican government."

"Why Five Guys?" I then asked.

"So, that was your dog that attacked me and stole my hamburger?" he asked.

"Yes."

"When you do this as often as I do, expediting my order is crucial. My food is normally ready for me every time I walk through those doors. The time your dog caught me in the parking lot, a new employee had messed up my order so I had to wait, which put me about ten minutes behind schedule. I thought I would miss the train connection. I wasn't too happy to say the least."

"Why then do you spend all the extra gas driving a truck when you could simply drive a car to collect the cases?" I asked.

"You've thought this through, haven't you?" Phillip said

recognizing Caroline's attention to details.

"I have had plenty of time to think about it, Phillip."

"We decided early on that we didn't want anyone to question why a delivery truck would deliver to an individual. No one ever sees a delivery truck stopping to personally deliver beverages to an individual. We chose the ballpark because it was easy access onto the highway and just two blocks from Phillip's normal route. It looks like a simple exchange of soda from one truck to another. No one has ever questioned us on it, until now," Henry answered with a smile.

"Wow," I said in amazement of what I had just heard. "What about the chemist? He must be frustrated with the lack of support here in the states."

"He is, but he's dealing with it. He plans to retire at the end of the trial. He'll receive full benefits from Rio Cola. I believe the Mexican government has agreed to retain him down there once he retires."

"Can anyone drink this cola, or is only for people with the specific illness?" I then asked. At this point, I was more interested in a product, a soft drink no less, that could actually be used for healing purposes.

"Yes, Caroline, anyone can drink it. That is what is so amazing about this product. It's a natural product. Not only can it be used to heal people with the precise disease, it acts as a deterrent for healthy people to prevent the disease from materializing."

"One more question," I then asked. "Why, Phillip, do you time your stops so precisely? You're not trying to meet a train."

"Awe, that's an easy question," Phillip teased. "There is a school around the corner from one of my stops. If I go too soon, I get stuck in traffic with a bunch of high school kids trying to rush to campus at the very last minute. Being stuck in the school traffic adds five or six minutes to my day. In addition, there is a factory that changes shifts about the same time I drive by. The traffic is really heavy there for about fifteen minutes as well. If I time everything perfectly, I can avoid the extra traffic that saves me nearly twenty minutes each day. Who doesn't want an additional twenty minutes to their day? We try to time it perfectly so Henry doesn't have to wait for me and I don't' have to wait for him. He can then get back to El Paso in time for his delivery."

"It sounds to me like you two are transporting million dollar beverages that are completely undetected by the human eye. I actually thought you might be transporting illegal drugs camouflaged as Rio-Cola. I'm glad to hear that everything you are doing is completely legal."

"It is Caroline. We would never do anything illegal," Phillip commented.

"I am concerned about your predicament," Henry stated. "Somebody knew that Phillip was driving that route daily, and that he came through at a certain time each day. I hope that doesn't mean we are being traced."

"Maybe you guys should change your meeting location, and get new cell phones," I suggested. "Do you think any of this would have anything to do at all with Calvin?"

"I'm not sure," Henry stated. 'It sounds like the investigation may not have been carried out to the fullest by your local

165

police."

"I agree," Phillip added. "I haven't shared this with any-one because I didn't think there was any correlation. I do know that Quinn is waiting for us to pick her up. She said you were planning to have us over to show us your place for the wedding. We'll be back in about forty-five minutes with some pizza. Let's just pretend that we were never here. Okay?"

After the brothers walked out, I hid the evidence of their visit by placing their glasses in the dishwasher. It didn't take long for the doorbell to ring again.

Chapter Fourteen

RAIN DROPS
AND ROSE PETALS

The hot breezy morning darkened as the storm clouds rolled across the plains into Albuquerque. A mist rose from the ground creating a haze that covered the land, disseminating visibility to a minimal. The horses across the street were no longer prancing through the fields. Once palpable, only outlines of their bodies remained.

I slumped down into my chair hugging my decorative pillow, overwhelmed by the pressure created by myself to make every moment of everyday perfect, for the next eight days. I had already failed. I couldn't muster enough energy to walk seven steps across the room to pick up a wad of dog fur near the leg of the chair. I kicked off my sandals and crawled into a ball to hide my face under my pillow.

I could feel the aches in my thighs and calves. "Where is my energy?" I whispered to myself. Maybe the late nights and early mornings that I had tackled for the past several weeks were gifting me with a cold. My head pounded and my eyes drooped; surely a sinus headache.

I had survived the workweek, completing a set for an upcoming film before its deadline, knowing my vacation was just around the corner. Michelle's eight weeks of wedding preparation had dwindled to four. Phillip's sister, the one from San Bernardino, could not make the original wedding date. Her children had obligations. Their spring break would start this week, just like my nephews' break. The wedding was moved forward to next Friday.

I looked at my watch with one eye barely open to see that three hours remained before the expected arrival of my family. They were scheduled to arrive at ten this morning, but their plane was diverted to Amarillo, Texas, a four-hour road trip away. Instead of delaying the arrival into Albuquerque, the airline chose to continue its flight into San Diego, its final destination while offering Albuquerque passengers the opportunity to exit in Amarillo, the nearest airport. The mountainous region of Santa Fe wasn't conducive to air travel either. Both airports had closed, something that rarely happened in this part of the country.

The airline offered the passengers two options, if they chose to exit the plane. They could be lodged in a local hotel over night awaiting a new flight the next day or they could be bussed to New Mexico. My family opted to board the Grey Hound. Rachel's kids had never been on a bus before and were anxious to experience something new for the first time. Their rental car, a mini van, would be waiting for them at the airport rental lot, one of three locations where the Greyhound planned to stop upon its arrival into Albuquerque. The delay would cost them an additional five extra hours of travel, but it was their best alternative.

I dozed off for a few minutes while lounging in the chair when I was startled by Lucy's bark. I jumped up from my slouched position to see the mail carrier pulling away from my mailbox at the end of my driveway. I guess Lucy had done her job. She chased the truck away. Maybe it was time for some ibuprofen. I walked into the kitchen, snatched a few bites of cheese and crackers, and then guzzled enough water to swallow the pills.

Slowly, I sauntered down the hallway to find my bed. I convinced Lucy to go outside one last time before the heavy rains fell. She didn't like rain. She hid from it whenever possible. She ran to the dog run, and raced back inside as quickly as possible. I don't remember how long it took for me to fall asleep again, perhaps thirty seconds. My eyelids were heavy and painful. With little effort, they fell down over my eyes, then opened again for a split second or two, before closing uncontrollably for the remainder of the afternoon.

Alarmed again, this time by the sound of my cell phone, my sister's voice could be heard loud and clear when I touched the screen of my phone. "Caroline, are you home? We've been ringing the doorbell for the past five minutes."

"Oh, you have?" I said. "Yea, I'll be right out. I fell asleep and never heard the bell." It occurred to me as I lethargically walked down the hall towards the front door that I was a heavy sleeper. Still yawning, I opened the door to a flock of boisterous youngsters. My sister, her husband, and my dad were standing patiently behind them, waiting to come inside. Unlike the others, my mom was still sitting in the middle row of the van not wishing to get wet by the downpour. I dug for an umbrella in the front closet and ran it out to her as everyone else rushed in.

"Come on in, mom. Welcome to my new home."

"If I had known the weather was going to be this bad, I would have stayed in Wisconsin," she announced.

"Oh, it's only going to be bad for a day," I said knowing that this was the worst storm we had encountered in years. "I'm really glad to see you, mom." I then hugged her as we walked inside.

By the time we got to the door, the kids had already run to the back of the house to see the pool.

"Mom. Dad. You have to see this," River called out through the house to his parents.

Doug could be heard above the chatter of everyone, "We're coming River."

Although the kids were profoundly disappointed that they could not swim now, they were elated to see the pool and waterfall.

"Just wait till you see the pool at night with the lights on," I told the kids. "You'll want to swim every night before going to bed. I'm not going to turn them on with the storm, though. You'll have to wait until tomorrow to see them."

"Dad," I continued, "I know you are hungry and tired from traveling, but would you be interested in helping me make some pizza? All of the ingredients are prepared and the dough has been rising all afternoon."

Our family had a tradition that had been going on for years. Anytime we gathered for a reunion, we always ate grandpa's pizza for our first meal together. Dad had the magic touch that no one had yet to perfect. It didn't matter how hard we tried, he could roll and knead the dough flawlessly giving life to the pizza crust making it irresistible.

"Doug, I'm down to just one car now. Just a few weeks ago my lease expired on the Land Rover. I turned it in, and traded Cal's car for something new. There's only one car parked in the garage now. If you want to unload out of the rain, you're welcome to pull the van into the garage. Boys, go help your dad bring in your luggage while your mom and I help grandpa make some pizzas. Okay?"

I quickly showed everyone where they would be sleeping for the next week. I gave mom and dad the guest room over looking the waterfall and pool deck. It was smaller than the front two guest rooms, but the view was spectacular. I had offered my room to them, but they refused. Rachel and Doug took the guest room looking out towards the Arabians while Reed & Claire chose the room next to them. The two older boys, Remington and River, seized the opportunity to sleep on the pullout in the family room. They liked the idea that they could watch television on a big screen while in bed.

As usual, dad's pizza was the best I had eaten since Christmas. It was a win-win meal for everyone. Remi always blanketed his pizza with pepperoni so there was not a single grate of cheese visible. He had been doing this since he was three. River always topped his pizza with sausage before layering a few pieces of pepperoni on top. Reed preferred an all meat pizza loaded with sausage, pepperoni, bacon and ham. Little Claire never really cared what ingredients were on her pizza as long as they formed a smiley face.

Love and laughter filled my home once again as the night faded away earlier than usual to the sound of rain tapping on the roof. I had a house full of weary travelers, and a sinus headache to dismiss.

I woke the next day to the rays of the early morning sun. My headache was gone. Birds were singing wildly, and earthworms mottled the pool deck everywhere. I began a fresh brew of coffee that Rachel brought with her before heading outside to begin the long process of cleaning the pool after the rain. I knew the kids couldn't get in it soon enough, so I was up early while everyone else slept.

I skimmed the debris out of the pool, and turned the jets on high allowing the filtering system to circulate the water more rapidly than normal. I manually vacuumed the bottom of the pool, leaving it spotless. The sun would dry out the pool deck and lawn furniture rather quickly I thought, but not soon enough to serve breakfast outdoors. I had already prepared quiche earlier in the week that I placed in the oven to warm.

When I was finished, I went back inside where I listened to the quiet giggling of the older boys in the adjacent room when I carried two bags of oranges from the pantry refrigerator to the kitchen counter. As discreetly as possible, I began cutting the oranges in half and placing them one at a time onto the electric juicer. Slowly the oranges lost their shape as the juice trickled into a clear canister leaving it's protective shell behind. The newly squeezed juiced registered one ounce, then two, three, and four. By the time I was done, forty-two ounces of sweet smelling citrus filled the air along with freshly brewed hazelnut coffee.

My attention wondered momentarily as I bagged the remains of the fruit to place in the garbage. I had a strange thought as I picked up the empty shell of an orange. Our lives, on a small scale, aren't so different than oranges. We live amidst our family, protected as children, until we are ripe and mature enough to leave home. We fall from the tree, or in some cases plucked. We are then put on display during the prime of our lives just as an orange awaits its homecoming in a fruit market or grocery store. Eventually, our coverings become prodded or bruised. When this happens, like the blade entering an orange, our souls overflow, leaving- in most cases- a tasteful outcome.

As quickly as that thought entered my mind, I was brought back to reality.

"Aunt Caroline," I heard the soft voice of Claire say, "When's Uncle Calvin coming home?"

"Do you want to come out to the pool with me, Claire?" I responded. "Then we can talk."

I quickly checked the timer on the oven to see that the quiche still had another ten minutes to go before it would be ready to eat. I grabbed two pool towels from the back hall, and escorted my darling niece outside with a cup of orange juice for both of us.

"Let's sit over here," I said as I laid two towels in the sun on the ground near the waterfall.

"Okay," Claire said as she followed me to a warm spot in the sun. "My mom told me not to talk about Uncle Calvin, but I want to know where he is," she innocently asked.

"That's alright," I told her. "We can talk about uncle Calvin if you like."

I then placed her small hand into the palm of my hand after she took a drink of her juice, and looked straight into her beautiful blue eyes.

"Young lady," I said, "sometimes things happen in life that no one can explain. Grownups often have a way of creating problems that can't be fixed. Sometimes the problems are so big that many people get hurt. Uncle Calvin got stuck in someone's problem. We don't know whose, but he had to leave because of this big, big problem. We don't know where he is, but he's probably trying to fix the problem."

"Well, I really miss him," little Claire said. "He always picked me up, and made me laugh, and played games with me."

"I miss him too, Claire. And, I know he misses you. Just remember, there is one thing that will never change, Claire. You will always be his favorite niece. Don't grow up too fast, though, he won't want to miss it."

I then reached down and hugged her tiny little body.

As we walked back to the house after finishing our juice, I said, "We are going to have some fun this week. We are going to ride a pony across the street. When your brothers go to the ball game, I plan to take you to the zoo. Would you like that?"

"Oh, that's sounds like fun," her tiny voiced echoed.

"And, if the weather's nice, we will even go for a balloon ride. You can swim in the pool as much as you want. Plus, there's something special happening on Friday. Do you remember what's happening here?" I asked.

"Yes, my mom and I went shopping for a really cute dress. She said that I'm going to be a flower girl in your friend's wedding. I have to show you my dress. It's yellow."

"Okay. I can't wait to see it. Maybe you can show it to me after we eat breakfast. Are you hungry yet?" I asked.

"Yes, I'm starving," little Claire stated. "Remember to tell uncle Calvin that I miss him when you see him again."

"Oh, I will. I promise you that I will tell him as soon as I can."

If perfection is possible, the week that began in a dismal array of mush, claimed victory. The grounds swallowed every last drop of water supplying the necessary nourishment for the greens to display their utmost spectrum of color. I didn't know that grass could be this green in New Mexico.

My energy returned when my headache disappeared, allowing me to entertain with pleasure rather than obligation. Rachel's family enjoyed all the outings, making it a vacation never to be forgotten. We hiked in the mountains, took the kids horseback riding, and swam daily in the pool. My parents chose to stay firmly planted on solid ground with Claire as we took to the skies in a company balloon on Tuesday morning. I had given everyone the choice of going on a hot air balloon ride or taking the tramway over the Sandia Mountains. Everyone, except Claire, chose the balloon ride. Since my parents had been many times before they chose to stay with their granddaughter.

Yesterday, while the rental company set up chairs and a pergola for the wedding ceremony, my dad took Doug and the boys to Isotopes Park for a ball game. All three of the boys played Little League Baseball so this was an ideal outing for them. Claire wanted to see the penguins and zebras at the zoo. It was the perfect get away for the women of the house. When we arrived home, Michelle and her crew had transformed the yard into a beautiful sanctuary.

Michelle stayed true to her word by hiring the rental company and caterer to organize the ceremonial details. In addition to allowing the event to take place at my house, my only obligations were to host a very small bachelorette party and make sure Michelle arrived on time. Both were easy to accomplish. The bachelorette party had taken place two weekends prior to the wedding, and Michelle spent her last night as a single woman at my house.

Harrison, as I continued to call him, escorted the family members to their appropriate seats while Phillip escorted both mothers. When everyone was seated, Harrison stood under the pergola along side his brother who was sporting his newest pair of cowboy boots. I knew from my experience working for a production company that if the film crew had only captured the tips of his boots on film, a gal would already know that an irresistible sexy face was the only entity that could possibly be on the other end. His boots said it all.

I learned that night when Michelle brought the Terric brothers over to my house that Phillip's love for horses started across the street. He had spent seven years riding in those stables. He periodically volunteers there with the equestrian therapy program for children with disabilities.

"It's your turn to go," I whispered to Claire as she began tossing white rose petals onto the luscious green grass. Her soft yellow dress swayed back and forth as she slowly walked up towards the archway. When she found her mark in the grass, she stopped and turned around waiting for the ring bearer to follow. Phillip's youngest nephew, his sister's son, was given the honor.

"Nice job," I whispered again to Claire when I reached the end of the walkway.

The moment arrived when Michelle walked out of the house, on the arm of her father, and headed towards the altar as *Wedding Song* resonated through the air while being played by Phillip's sister on the keyboards. I had never seen Michelle more beautiful. Her gown was simple, with her shoulders barely covered, allowing unparalleled poise of her most prominent features. Her grace was rampant.

Their nuptials were heartfelt. I only wished Calvin could have been here.

The bride and groom danced into the early hours of the night, enjoying every moment of their reception. Little did they know that a surprise still a waited.

When the time came, I announced for everyone to join Phillip and Michelle across the street. I had arranged for Striking High's newest hot air balloon to carry the newlyweds above the countryside at sunset before heading to the city's outskirts to see the skyline at night. They would return to the company's airstrip where a limousine would take them to their honeymoon suite downtown. Their flight to Maui wasn't leaving until Saturday at noon.

When they waived goodbye, I knew I could finally relax.

Chapter Fifteen
PONDEROSA TRAIL

Ponderosa Trail boasted a little bit of everything. Trees, rocks, hills, plateaus, amazing views, and water encompassed an eight-mile loop that every mountain bicyclist could conquer. It was short enough that the novice could make an attempt at completing it, yet challenging enough to entice the return of moderate to advanced riders. I liked the trail because Lucy could run along side me and still find refuge from the heat.

With the eight-day whirlwind behind me, I would now focus on a new normalcy. As Michelle had experience when Cal and I first married, there was an adjustment period that I needed to overcome in finding a balance in our relationship. She wouldn't be able to stop over as frequently as before, and I wouldn't be able to drop over unannounced whenever I wanted.

It was a hard week at work, returning phone calls and addressing issues that I had missed while I was on my stay-at-home vacation. I did not have any immediate deadlines to accomplish, but was still exhausted from the nonstop pendulum of events. I had hoped to go mountain biking early this morning with riders from the club, but I failed to wake from my alarm. Instead, Lucy and I would spend the day together anticipating the return of the newlyweds tonight.

There were five cars in the dirt parking area when we arrived at the entrance to this trail. On most days there would have been twenty to thirty cars, but my late arrival had assured me that the diehard riders were gone by now. If I had come in July or August, Lucy would not have been able to survive the intense heat either, but it was still April when temperatures were manageable.

A silver Jeep Cherokee, a white Kia Rio with a roof carrier, a red Honda Element, a blue Nissan Cube, and a green Ford Fiesta with a back rack were parked in a row. I was driving my new scarlet Jeep Wrangler with a factory fitted bike carrier on the back. I pulled up under a tree away from the line of cars.

I unloaded my red Trek Fuel EX that had adequate suspension for trail rides here in New Mexico. It wasn't the absolute best mountain bike built, but was close to being the best. I actually preferred the suspension on this bike better. I didn't anticipate the need to repair any flat tires, but I always rode prepared. I strapped several water bottles to my waste along with protein bars, my cell phone and signal boosters, and my repair kit. In addition, my new Jeep was equipped with an auxiliary antenna to help capture a better cellular signal. Since Cal's disappearance, I have tried to better prepare myself in case of an emergency. I have since kept a supply of dog food and extra clothing with me in my vehicle as well. I never leave home without a cooler full of ice, beverages, and some food.

The sun was high when Lucy and I took off down the trail. She knew that she needed to stick close by me to help avoid any unwelcome rattlesnakes. She had seen a few snakes in her days, and discovered that they were not the friendliest of friends. We both knew that the best defense against them was to stay away. They would not bother us, if we didn't bother them.

Mountain biking was completely different from road cycling. I had learned over the years that the key to successful off road riding was to know my limitations. Working with the terrain rather than against it always helped prevent tumbles. Unlike some of my friends who were much more experienced than me, I erred on the side of caution. I preferred safety to exhilaration.

I took it easy when Lucy and I first began. I needed my muscles to loosen up before I attempted any jumps or extensions. The trail was perfect for this because it was rather flat at the beginning and free of trees and boulders. I peddled along turning in and out of the curves as they approached. Lucy followed about five feet behind me, staying on the trails rather than wandering off.

I remembered camping along the shores of Lake Michigan many times as a kid, and finding it difficult for Rachel and me to ride our bikes in the sand. Our wheels would spin beneath us, not allowing us to ride very far until we found firmer ground. The desert sand on these trails was more tightly packed making it easier to navigate.

A mile or so down the path, the trail wove through a section of trees casting shadows everywhere. This was one of my favorite sections of the course. Dodging fallen trees and making hairpin turns while maintaining a decent pace was challenging. I was forced to come to a halt when a half a century old Rio Grande cottonwood blocked the lane. Its trunk was almost four feet wide.

I unclipped my toe clips and dismounted from my bike. I lifted my bike high over my head so the bottom side of my wheels would clear the tree. I tossed it over so that it landed derailleur side up. I didn't want the weight of my bike to break the derailleur if it had hit the ground. Since I was already off my bike, I decided to take a short water break. I knew I would be taking one again soon, but I rarely stopped in this section of the trail.

The next time I would come through here, the fallen tree would likely already be cut by a chain saw opening up the path again. Park rangers came through once every month or two to free fallen debris if it was too large for the average person to conquer. I know quite a few guys from the bike club, including Joshua and Jason, who would have been able to cross this tree without ever getting off their bikes. Not me, I didn't have a chance in the world.

Lucy jumped up onto the trunk of the tree with me. I took a drink from my bottle and squirted some into her mouth before walking down the trunk as far as I could with my arms guiding me like the wings of a plane. I could almost hear the voice of Rachel saying, "Caroline, look at me." I turned around thinking she might actually be there with me. I reminisced of our childhood days.

"Okay, let's go Lucy," I said when I mounted my bike again. It was a short ride through the remainder of the wooded area that egressed to a rocky area. I spent much of the next phase of the ride standing up on my pedals as I negotiated the large rocks and boulders that led down to the water basin. I rode slow using my brakes frequently to balance my load as I stepped down from boulder to boulder until I reached the valley floor. It would have been much easier to get off my bike and walk, but that would not have been challenging.

This was Lucy's favorite part of the trail. She immediately ran down to the creek and splashed around. I again got off my bike and leaned it up against a boulder. I went down to the water's edge and stepped from rock to rock across the stream. I skipped a few stones that Lucy tried to retrieve. Never being able to find the actual one that I threw, she always came back with something in her mouth.

When Lucy was done playing, she drank from the stream then found a rock to lie on to rest. I sat down next to her to give her a few treats while I ate a protein bar. I could see further down the way a young couple who were soaking their feet in the water. I was too far away to talk to them, but it was nice to know that there were other people out here too.

The next part of the ride was the most difficult. I needed to climb a plateau before reaching the trail again. I would not clip my bike shoes into the straps because I would be on and off my bike a dozen times before reaching the trail. I always cycled with my clips tightened to allow better leverage and maneuvering. I rested my bike on my shoulder as I stepped across the rocks trying to prevent falling into the stream.

I mounted my bike and rode about fifty yards before I had to make my first ascent. I once again placed my bike on my shoulder as I climbed several feet before placing my bike on a ledge that was about five feet wide. Lucy climbed part way up, and then I boosted her back end to help her scale the remaining couple of feet.

This process continued for about twenty minutes as Lucy and I made our way up to the top of the gorge. We took another water break when we reached the top. I had a fold-up camping cup that I used for Lucy. I took it out of my pack and poured several ounces of water into her dish. She drank it all.

The next section of the park took us again through some rocky terrain before reaching another wooded area. The trees on this side of the ravine were less dense than the other, but I still coveted retreat from the sun. This section was covered with Pinon trees, Hackberry trees, and desert willow trees. The willow trees had not come into blossom yet, but would be showcasing their bell-shaped flowers soon.

Lucy could easily keep up with me during this part of the ride. The trail had fewer turns and was less drooling for any rider. As we approached the clearing, I could see a flock of birds feasting on the fruit of some New Mexico olive trees about a hundred yards from the trail. We still had about a mile to go before reaching the Jeep.

When we reached the sunlight again, the heat intensified against my already warm body. I was now looking forward to my return home where I planned to swim and lounge out by the pool for the remainder of the day. When we were about a half-mile from the lot, a swarm of tiny desert gnats covered the trail. I tucked my head and powered through them hoping they were the non-biting kind. Lucy was low enough to the ground that she ran underneath them without any problems. A few of them stuck to the sweat on my arms, but I managed to fly through them without any entering my mouth. I was unscathed.

I could see a number of vehicles in the parking area as Lucy and I returned from our trek. The Jeep Cherokee and red Honda Element were still there along with two different vehicles that parked on the opposite side of the lot. A Ford Taurus was parked near the entrance with its windows down while a white Chrysler Pacifica parked across from the Honda. I typically don't pay much attention to vehicles in a parking lot, but it's hard not to notice them when they are parked out here away from civilization.

I rode up behind my Jeep where I dismounted to unlock the door. I was really glad that I parked under the tree today since it was providing a little shade. Without looking at my watch, I could tell by the shadows on the ground that it must have been around one o'clock. I fumbled through my waist pack to find my key fob as Lucy waited for a bowl of ice-cold water. I always packed two extra Tupperware bowls for her that I kept in the cooler. After opening the tailgate, I pulled a bowl out for her and a water bottle for me. I then shut the door to load my bike onto the back rack.

I stood momentarily with my head tilt back drinking the cold water. It tasted good. The refreshing wetness coated my mouth and tongue making it easier to swallow. My mouth was parched from the long ride. The unused water that I still had in my second bottle was too hot to drink. I reached down and untied my cleats as Lucy continued to drink from her bowl. I took each shoe off and tossed them along with my socks onto the floor of the back seat while I slipped into my flip-flops. I was anxious to get home now.

As I began to reach for Lucy's empty bowl, she growled unlike any I had ever heard from her before. When I turned to look behind me in the direction she was barking, I felt a tremendous pain in my right arm. I caught the glimpse of a man's arm and black mask as I fell forward into the opened door. I tried to move, but felt dizzy as my head spun into a world of darkness.

Chapter Sixteen
THE LETTER

The page in front of me was still blank as I struggled to write the letter. I was still trying to figure out what had happened to me "That's it," I exclaimed to myself. I was reaching down to pickup Lucy's bowl when she started barking. I immediately started to panic. What did they do to my dog? Is she okay? She can't survive in the desert without food and water. Is someone taking care of her? Did anyone find my Jeep? Surely, Michelle and Phillip would notice there was a problem when I didn't pick them up at the airport. What happened to my cell phone?

I then looked down at my arm and noticed a small lump where I had been injected. I had definitely been drugged. I looked around the room again, but found no signs of my waist pack or my phone. The door was still locked and I was still stuck. I reread the note again. *You have thirty-six hours from now to draft a farewell letter to your parents. You will not be seeing them again. If you say anything about your location or how you got here, there will be consequences. If you choose to cooperate, you will be reunited with your husband.*

I was still shocked and upset, but I knew that I was really left with no choice. If I would not be seeing my parents again, I certainly wanted to see Calvin. Here it goes, I thought.

SAYING GOODBYE

Dear Mom & Dad,

I can't begin to tell you how much I enjoyed your company last week. Although it was action packed, I could not have asked for a better week. It was therapeutic for me to have the entire family in my new home. I was anxious to begin my new life, putting the past behind me, and moving forward with a hope for a better tomorrow.

As I have already shared with you, I have no idea how my life or Cal's lead up to the predicament in which we found ourselves seven short months ago. I have since discovered, against my desires, another predicament in which I have no control. I have been given an ultimatum to send a farewell letter to you.

From all practical perspectives, it now appears that Cal is alive, as I had predicted all along. For me to see him again, I must chose between you and him. How does a daughter ever choose to say goodbye to her parents? It was never suppose to be this way. I have spent the last several hours contemplating the consequences of my actions. There is no easy answer. I don't want to lose you, nor am I ready to lose him. Please understand that this decision is not one based on false pretense.

I have lived apart from you for the past decade of my life. Calvin has been the foundation from which my adult life has been built. I cannot turn my back on him now. Likewise, I know you would not want me to turn my back on him, but to pursue the truth of his disappearance and whereabouts.

You have one another to hold tight, and Rachel has her family. I have no one. I need to see my husband again, even if it's for just a brief time. So, if this is 'Saying Goodbye,' please know that I say it with a burden too heavy to hold, a love too magnificent to fathom, and a heart too swollen to break.

Thank you from the depths of the deepest ocean and the height of the tallest mountain for allowing me to be me, and for loving me unconditionally. Don't let your hearts be troubled, but be humbled in knowing that I will have life again. May you find forgiveness in the lives of those who have walked in this stealthy way. And, may you love for all eternity. Please don't ever give up hope.

Until we meet again, your daughter's love overflows.

I love you mom & dad!

Caroline

Well, I did it. I wrote the letter. What happens next? What happens if my family tries to find me? The questions returned, agitating my mind like rocks being polished in a tumbler. Maybe I need to write a letter that is more brisk, to the point, one with specific detailed information. I'm sure someone will read the letter so maybe I just need to be discreet, providing hints that only my family would know.

I looked down on the desk again. I still had two sheets of blank paper left. I walked to the window and gazed out upon the waters. There is so much I want to say. I have to try again. There is no doubt that my mom and dad will immediately call Rachel who will come to analyze the letter with them. I have to try another approach.

SAYING GOODBYE

Dear Mom & Dad,

"Saying Goodbye" isn't something I thought I would ever need to do. I have stumbled into a situation with very few choices. I have been given the task of sending a farewell letter to you for the exchange of my husband. At least, that is what they presented to me. I am well and safe, and not lacking anything. Matter of fact, I was given a caramel penlight this morning after being awakened by the sunlight.

As I ponder over and over again what to do or say, I am reminded of my childhood, and the plans Rachel and I conceived. Our dreams for tomorrow are so far away now. I don't regret any of those times. They were beautiful. And, I cherish the most recent days we spent together as a family. It was wonderful being together again.

I am not sure how I got here, or how anyone gets to where they are going. I just know that we still need to drink the water, or in your case dad, the cola. The sun still rises in the east and sets in the west no matter where we live.

Mom, please don't cry. You have been amazing, loving, and caring for years. I couldn't have asked for a better mother. You are my hero. If I had known a week ago what I know today, I would have encouraged all of us to take the flight. Claire would have loved the ride. Please tell her that I am keeping my promise to her about uncle Cal. She will know what that means.

There is one thing I have learned over the past seven months. Time is precious. Cherish each moment, making it the best it can be. One day at a time is sufficient. One hour at a time is even better. Don't wish for tomorrow. It may bring sorrow too enormous to comprehend. Live for today, Tomorrow may drift away before it has time to reach you.

I want to leave you with one last thought. Love is unconditional. It doesn't disappear because someone forces unwanted change. As long as you are alive, my love dwells within you, keeping you alive. As long as I am alive, your love lives within me, keeping me alive as well. Please give my love to the family. I love all of you more than words can ever express. I am thankful for each of you too. Despite the recent events, life has been good. Don't let that change.

Overflowing with all our love, I love you to the Caroline Star and back.

Your Daughter, Caroline

P.S. Tell all the kids they are welcome to swim in my pool anytime, but not Harrison's older brother.

I folded both letters and put them separately in the two envelopes. I debated whether or not I should seal the envelopes. If I sealed them, they might tear them open and never send them. At this point, I anticipated that the letters would be read regardless. I kept them open. I addressed both of them to an address in Wind Point, north of Racine. It was my grandmother's home. She passed away a year and a half ago.

She lived in a cottage on Lake Michigan. No one lives there now. The cottage had seen better days, but my dad had been fixing the place up. My mom commented to me just last week that she should have the mail forward to their house. My parent's name, number, and address have never been in the phone book. Even as a kid, our number was always unlisted. I never thought to ask them about it.

I'm not really sure when the thirty-six hour clock began. Did it start when I arrived last night? I don't even know when I arrived. I think yesterday was Saturday, but I don't know for sure how long I was out. If my thirty-six hours started last night, then it must be done by morning. If it started this morning, then I probably still have another twenty-five or twenty-six hours to go. Will I get to see Calvin sooner if I give them the letters sooner?

I was being over analytical now. Trust wasn't a virtue that any of my captors had acquired. I shouldn't believe a word they say. I sat down again to reread the letters once more. It was nearing six o'clock. At least I thought it must be nearing six, based on the tide outdoors. What does it matter if I say goodbye to my parents anyway? If they wanted a ransom for me, wouldn't they approach my parents? None of this made any sense.

I changed my mind again. I would moist just the very center of the envelope with tap water to make it stick. It would prevent the letters from falling out, yet allow them to open easily if the guys wanted to read them. I contemplated for several more minutes, deliberating whether the letters were good enough or when I should place them outside my door.

I had one more piece of paper left. I could always write a third letter if there was something important that I failed to say in the first two letters. Or, I could use it to make a paper airplane to help pass the time.

I read both letters over a fourth time while sitting on the

191

bed. I then sealed each of them with a soft kiss before placing them back into the envelopes. I walked over to the bathroom sink, and dabbed a drop of water on my index finger to dab the glue at the center of the envelope. I walked up to the door, and gently placed them underneath. I had done my part. Now it was up to them.

Dinner arrived about a half hour later, and still my captors did not speak a word. I ran to the door when I heard the door unlock, but it was too late. I had been sitting by the window watching the waves crash against the beach. A solid white pizza box had quickly been placed on the floor inside my room.

"Hey," I shouted. "Who are you? What do you want from me?" I pounded on the door in frustration, but no one responded. I could only hear the steps of a person walking down the hall. My door was locked again.

I wasn't sure if the box was a teaser or if pizza was actually inside. I was happy to find a steaming hot pizza prepared with fresh mushrooms, Italian sausage, pepperoni, sweet onion and oregano. Again, I was given food that I liked, but I had no idea how anyone could know that this was my favorite type of pizza. I was puzzled once more. Whoever these people were, they were going out of their way to prepare meals that I truly enjoy without providing any additional clues.

I grabbed the box and a cold Rio-Cola out of the refrigerator, and then headed to the window to sit and watch the waves. I wasn't expecting to see anything new as I ate my pizza, but I had nothing better to do.

It must have been around five thirty or so. I could tell because the water now crept higher and higher upon the beach slowly as the tide stretched forth its hand striving to reach something it could not have. All daylong it had continued to reach forward, occasionally snagging a piece of driftwood, seaweed, or shell fragments, and pulling it back to itself.

Now it was able to reach just a little further. Day after day, week after week, and year after year, this ocean and every ocean calls, but they all stop when their boundaries draw near. I never thought about this before, until today. All the seas have boundaries. When I think of the ocean, I typically think of it from my position, standing on land. If you look at it from their perspectives, out in the water, the oceans can only reach the beaches. They must stay off the land where people roam and buildings stand. On rare occasion, a few find a way to invite themselves onto uncharted territory. When they do, all havoc breaks lose. They become our worst enemies.

I then reminisced about Rachel and me when we sailed on Lake Michigan as kids. When we were out on the water, I always felt like I we were on the ocean. There were many times when we were out so far that we could not see land. It wasn't until I was older that I learned how vastly different the oceans are from the Great Lakes.

Tonight, the ocean would again be my friend. I tried to let it lure me back to sleep after dinner. After some tossing and turning from me, I gave in to the night. I was restless and could not sleep. Without a television, radio, computer, telephone, or book, my options for entertainment were limited. I still had the one piece of paper. I could use it to write some notes, or another letter. If I stayed here too much longer, I might need to use the walls for my paper. That would be a sight.

I decided the only thing left to do was exercise. I think I spent around an hour exercising, the old fashion way. I crawled down onto the carpet, and stretched for a very long time, maybe thirty minutes, before I began a set of pushups, sit-ups, and crunches. My arm was sore from the injection, but I needed something to do. I did the routine again for another thirty minutes until I couldn't do another pushup. I stretched a second time and pretended to do some yoga. I had never participated in any yoga classes, but I had seen enough of them at the gym that I remembered a few things. I closed my eyes, took a deep breath, and exhaled. I mediated for a few minutes and said a quick prayer for the first time in years, "God, please help me."

When I was done, I opted for another shower. I locked the bathroom door, and went through the same ritual that I had done earlier in the day to secure the door. I still couldn't trust anyone.

Chapter Seventeen
BARGAIN DAY

During the silence of the dawn, the waves continued to crash steadily onto the beach as the sun awakened from its sleep casting light across the top of each billow. A dark rhythm of light appeared on the wall dancing to the beat of each wave through a reflection from the mirror. It caught my attention as I slowly lifted my head from the feathers on which I slept. I yawned twice and laid back down. The room was still dark.

When the reflection grew brighter, I crawled out of bed and strolled over to the chair by the window to watch as the crust of the sun slowly lifted above the horizon. As I sat gazing across the ocean, I saw a black shadow rise on the earth's surface. It was a freighter. It progressed so slowly that it looked like it was standing still. Yet, I knew it wasn't. Affixed to that one object, I watched for twenty minutes before it vanished out of sight.

The headache that taunted me yesterday was completely gone. I felt much better than I did twenty-four hours ago. The moderate exercise last night helped. If only I could find a way to execute a cardiovascular work out, that would greatly help too.

After the sun gleamed in its fullness, I turned around in the chair to ponder what I might do next. It was then that I noticed a bag of clothes inside the door. I had not heard the door open nor had I seen the bag when I first woke up. I jumped out of the chair and ran to get the bag. I quickly looked inside to find my extra set of clothes that I had placed in the Jeep. "Yes," I thought to myself. I can wear something more comfortable today. I held my clothes up to my face and took a deep breath. "Awe," I exclaimed, the smell of home.

My running shoes, two clean pairs of footies, a brush, and an extra pair of underwear were in my bag along with a pack of gum. I was like a little girl opening her gifts at Christmas. I savored each moment as I lifted the items from the bag.

Trying to put some order back into my life when there is nothing to do is challenging. Since I had no idea how long I would be trapped here and Cal had already been missing for seven months, I thought I should plan for the long haul. I decided that I would begin each morning with stretching and a shower before breakfast, if they continued to feed me. I changed out of the robe that I wore to bed and back into my bike clothes. I didn't want to get my clean clothes dirty from exercise.

I sat back down on the floor to stretch, facing the bathroom. As I gazed across the room while I began my stretches, I realized that I could get my heart pumping after all. That bathroom tub was high enough that I could use it for step-ups. At that moment I remembered that the football players in my high school used to do them on the bleachers. I finished my stretches then slowly placed my socks and running shoes on my feet. I then tied my shoes, using Shep's method.

When Rachel and I were young, our dad taught us a different way to tie our shoes. He had a client who served in the United States armed forces as a green beret. There he learned to tie his shoes with a double knot that had two separate knots for

196

each lace. Most people tie a single knot for both laces, then add an additional knot to the one already tied. Shep's way allowed each lace to be individually knotted, which prevented the lace from untying on its own accord. I have never had my shoes come untied using Shep's method.

When I was done tying my shoes, I walked into the bathroom and stepped up onto the tub, one foot at a time. I started slow to warm up, not to injure myself and to get a feel for this type of exercise. Although I had seen it done many times before, it wasn't the type of physical activity I was used to doing. It took a couple of minutes for me to settle into a rhythm.

Now, I needed to keep the beat going. My only view was that of the parrot and pineapple on the wall. Seeing them over and over again became monotonous, so I decided to focus on music. I would try to recall every lyric to as many songs as possible to pass the time away. I wanted to give up about five minutes after I started, but I knew that I couldn't allow myself to fail. I kept going. I would need to think of at least five songs to stretch this exercise out for twenty minutes. If I liked it well enough, I might need to do it twice a day.

Once I got the hook of it, the time flew by as I mentally engaged in music that jarred my memory. Sweat poured down my face as it had when I was abducted. I didn't mind sweating when exercising, but any other time meant that it was an unpleasant thing… anxiety, stress, nervousness, or sizzling temperatures. This was a good sweat.

I checked my heart rate when I was finished, and walked around the room for a few minutes before showering. Once I completed the ritual of barricading the door, I stepped foot into the shower once again. The water was cooler than the previous showers that I had taken, as the first drops rolled down my right ankle and then onto my face as I stepped under the showerhead. After bathing and washing my hair, I turned the faucet to the right to turn up the heat. I then stood motionless pondering the possible scenarios that I hoped I would encounter today.

I had decided the night before that I would try my best to remain positive regardless of the outcome. If I could be optimistic, then I had a better chance of surviving this ordeal. I had kept my end of the deal by writing the letter, so I was planning on them keeping their bargain. I still had no idea why they would want me to say goodbye to my parents.

After standing in the shower for several more minutes, the fresh scent of the soft towel felt comforting as I dried my face, arms, and the rest of my body. I then place my arms and head through the openings of my shirt, smelling another fresh scent that reminded me of home. Needless to say, I felt more energized now than I did earlier.

When I opened the door of the bathroom, a new aroma filled the air. A ham, cheese, and mushroom omelet oozing with steam sat on a plate along with a mini bagel, butter and cream cheese. A small cup of fresh fruit accompanied the meal. I was vaguely surprised to find fresh pineapple in the assortment. That is a rarity with most establishments, but one that I utterly enjoyed. A glass of ice water and cranberry juice filled two goblets as well.

I was so busy eating my breakfast that I barely noticed a note that was left partially beneath my plate on the tray. As with the first note, it was typed on plain paper.

"Your door will be unlocked at 10:00 am. Wait 5 minutes. Go down the hall to the stairs. At the bottom, turn left, and then proceed through the great room to the doors leading to the beach. You may walk the beach. Do not open any doors or walk into any other part of the house. If you do, there will be consequences. Further instructions will be given to you later."

I quickly ran to the window to look outside. It was exactly the same as it had been every time I looked out the window. It was desolate. The sea breeze blew against the sand grasses causing them to lean towards the house while the waves continued to crash onto the shore. The wetness of the sand would ebb for a brief second only to be submerged again by an oncoming wave. The sun was higher in the sky now. Based off of its location and my morning activities, I calculated the current time to be a few minutes past eight, giving me nearly a two-hour window to formulate a plan.

I could feel my heart beat race as anxiety entered every inch of my body. The questions in my mind multiplied making any logical attempt to comprehend my situation even more complicated. I was searching for an exit strategy, one that would give me some type of control. The only power I had now in the confines of these four walls boiled down to eating, exercising, bathing, and meditating upon a vast sea with an endless sky. I couldn't even control my sleeping.

I looked around the room again to see if there was anything at all I could use to escape, as I pondered my best options. I still didn't know for sure where I was being held. Once outside, I had hoped the temperature, landscape, and details of the exterior of the home would help me determine a more specific location. I didn't know if I was miles from civilization or possibly on an island.

My captors had been non-confrontational and treated me quite well so far, except when they initially injected me. Would that change if I took off running down the beach or towards a road? Would they simply shoot me down? They certainly went to some effort to make me comfortable so far. I continued to search for a reasonable approach to find an end to my predicament.

Bed linens, towels, shampoo, soap, hairbrush, tooth paste and brush, light bulbs, lamps, and hardware from the dresser pulls... I went through every single item in the room trying to determine what alternative purpose each could possess. The options were so few that it didn't take long for me to device a plan.

I walked into the bathroom to get a clean white towel. If nothing else, I could use it as a beach towel without looking suspicious. While I was there I brushed my teeth, swishing the water around in my mouth several times before spitting it into the sink. I then rinsed my face by cupping my hands and splashing water into my eyes. I reached for a hand towel with my left hand as I look forward into the mirror. "Not bad," I thought, for a girl without makeup.

I wasn't the type of woman to coat layers and layers of foundation and makeup on my face. Nor, did I enjoy adding stroke after stroke of eye shadow or thicken my lashes to the point where they looked fake. I was a simple gal. A little eye shadow and liner, and some blush went a long way for me. I had a theory that women who covered their faces with product were actually bleaching their faces. Everyone I knew who glamorized themselves with any type of base always seemed to have very pale, ghostly skin without the makeup. I was convinced that the foundation was preventing sunlight and nutrients from replenishing natural tones that would otherwise be found.

After drying my face, I neatly folded the towel and placed it back onto the towel bar. I then grabbed a large towel along with my toothbrush and toothpaste. I walked across the room to the side table next to the upholstered chair. I unscrewed the light bulb. I could hide it easily enough under the towel without drawing attention to it. I placed these items on my bed.

Next, I sat down at the table to write one last note; four times. I folded the paper in fourths, creasing each edge before tearing it neatly along the edge of the desk. I was hoping I might be able to find a way to leave each note somewhere where people might find it. Each note was the same.

SOS. My name is Caroline Richards. I am 33 years old. I was kidnapped from Albuquerque, NM on Saturday, April 17, 2003. I have been confined to one room in a white 2-story beach house that faces the rising sun. I might be near South Padre Island in Texas or maybe even Flagler Beach in Florida. I don't know for sure. Please help me. Thank you.

I then took all four pieces of paper and folded them into small squares about two inches wide. I put three of the four into my pocket. The fourth one I set aside with the other items I would be taking with me.

I wasn't sure the exact time, but I thought I had about fifteen more minutes before the hour would arrive. I looked at my shoes and flip-flops. I wish I could just run out there barefoot and splash around in the water and not worry about tomorrow, let alone the next hour. My conscious told me to put on my socks and shoes again. I should be prepared for the unknown. Once again, I grabbed a clean pair of footies from my bag and placed them on my feet.

I took a bottled Rio Cola out of the refrigerator, drank a few sips, and placed it on the bed with my other items. I carefully examined the items I had thrown there. As much as I wanted to take the bag that my clothes came in, I decided that might look a bit suspicious. I needed to look like I was going to walk the beach, not run away. I would also leave the toothbrush and toothpaste. That left me with a towel, light bulb, chewing gum, and my four notes.

My mind was churning again. Did I really need the light bulb? My only thought was that it could be used for self-defense. I was being treated very well, so maybe the light bulb wouldn't be needed. I changed my mind, and replaced the bulb back into the socket on the lamp. I was going to make it simple… a beach towel, two pieces of gum, the notes, and soft drink.

I knew I was getting nervous because I had to use the bathroom again. I quickly got in and out of there and waited by the window once more. As I gazed outside, nothing had changed except the sun was higher in the sky than it was earlier.

I then heard a knock as a note was slid underneath the door. As I crossed the room to pick up the note, I could hear the key rattle, as the door was unlocked. I was excited. I wanted to race out of the room to see who was behind all of this non-sense, yet I didn't want to jeopardize any consequence. Like the previous notes, it was typed written and read, "Wait 5 minutes." It was that simple.

The footsteps vanished as they walked down the hall. I sat on the bed and waited patiently. I think I probably waited six or seven minutes before I actually stood up to leave. I grabbed the towel with one hand and the Rio Cola with the other. My fourth note was in the palm of my hand hidden against the bottle. While I was waiting I began chewing one piece of gum. The other I slid into my pocket with the other notes.

I couldn't believe how calm I actually was right now. I stood in front of the door, closed my eyes, and took a deep breath. I slowly opened the door a crack, half expecting to find a trap. It was clear. I walked down the hall trying to pay attention to the details.

The soft blonde floors were an engineered hardwood that met to a six-inch baseboard painted in a soft white color. The walls were a very subtle and welcoming yellow. My room was the farthest one to the north of the hall on the beach side. There were three doors on the right side of the hall, and only one more door on the left before reaching the top of the stairs.

Between my room and the other on the left was a large canvas painting of a young boy and girl playing with marbles. It was beautiful, but very odd for this place. I continued my walk down the stairs with one hand on the handrail where I turned left, as the instructions had indicated. It was still silent as I tip toed through the house.

The great room, as called in the note, was spectacular.

An extremely large white kitchen with a twelve-foot long island was to the far left. Six barstools facing the water lined the counter. A large twenty-foot dining table was engulfed in the center of the room. Six upholstered arm less chairs faced each other on both sides of the table. The host and hostess chairs, draped with a beautiful coral floral, were on each end complimenting the solid stripe found in each of the arm less chairs.

All three external walls were floor to ceiling windows. I had never been in a place quite like this one before. Too bad I couldn't be here with family and friends enjoying a get away. The interior wall that was beside the staircase was the only solid wall. I turned to see that a much larger canvas embraced the focal of that wall. A vibrant and colorful image of sailboats lined along a dock took me immediately back to Racine's waterfront. It was a magnificent painting.

I resumed my pilgrimage through the entertainment area of the great room towards the French doors. A large upholstered sofa faced the interior wall to my right where a flat screen hung from the melon colored wall. Planked on each side of the sofa were two more upholstered chairs. Behind the sofa stood a long and narrow table with a conch shell, piece of coral, and a starfish. Next to it was a coffee table book. I could not tell the name of the book, but the cover was several shades of blue.

A four-foot wide aisle formed between the sofa table and a row of five upholstered chairs which faced the water and beach. I walked passed the chair towards the doors, and was immediately overwhelmed with heat as I walked outside. It was at least seventy-five or six degrees outside, but the smell of the ocean breeze was exuberant.

I walked through some tall grasses scattered up and down the beach as I headed towards the ocean. It was probably around a hundred yards from the house to the edge of the water. I couldn't resist any longer. I needed to take off my shoes. I sat down on my towel for a few minutes while I untied my shoes. I took off my socks, keeping them right side out and tucked them inside each shoe. I then tied the laces of each shoe together so I could fling them over my shoulders allowing me to carry them hands free when I decided to walk down to the beach. I immediately jumped to my feet and ran into the water. It was warm, very warm.

I am sure I had eyes on me, watching my every move. I twirled around and splashed and pretended that it was the first time I had ever seen the beach. I acted like any young child who was seeing the ocean for the very first time. When I turned around to see the house, I was stunned at its size. It was larger than I had expected.

To the north, the closest house was probably a mile up the beach. Beyond that house, I did not see a single building or skyline. To the south, there were several houses, all located within a quarter of a mile from one another. They were much further down the beach, probably two miles away. I could see them because the beach turned slightly allowing them to be seen from afar.

After seeing the sand and feeling the water, I knew I was on the Gulf of Mexico. The water and waves were different from the Atlantic Ocean. I had to be close to South Padre Island. If not, I was somewhere along the Mexican coastline where civilization was nonexistent for miles.

I walked back to the sand where I dropped my shoes and socks, and sat down on my towel for a few minutes to dry off. As I sat there, I noticed that the wind was no stranger to the waves. It roared and shouted to the tune of a hollow drum, beating in rhythm endlessly without a cause. The waves were talking to each other like birds singing to one another after a mild rain or at the brisk of dawn. The sounds were as unique as any voice. Some were baritones while others were altos, but each one crashed and echoed as it carried itself onto the beach, foaming as it emptied onto the granular surface darkened by the moisture within it. Some of the waves were gaunt and fell short upon reaching their final destination onto dry land. Other waves sounded with a resonating splash like a child throwing a ball into a pool of water.

As I gazed out into the emptiness of the sea, I wondered why they had waited so long to let me out. Civilization was almost nonexistent, and transportation didn't appear to be available. Although the four walls were down, I still felt confined. My walls were no longer vertical, but horizontal - water to the east and sand to the west. I could walk, but I knew I would not get very far.

Chapter Eighteen
MY MESSAGE IN A BOTTLE

The warm soda didn't taste as good now as it had when I first opened it, so I poured the remaining beverage into the sand with my back still towards the house. I then rinsed the bottle with salt water and sat back down as I waited for the warm sun to dry out the bottle. After about fifteen minutes of sitting on the beach, I used the tip of my towel to dry out a few remaining drops of water inside the bottle.

I placed the fourth note inside the dry bottle knowing that my chances of anyone ever finding the note was about as good as counting all the stars in the sky. They would be impossible to count, and so were my chances of anyone finding this note. Instead of working on movie sets, my life had become a movie script. I couldn't write a better one if I had tried. With most movies there was always the hope of something magical happening in the final scene. For that reason alone, I decided to put one of my notes in the bottle. I could picture my camera crew now, even though I knew that daydreaming was a far cry from reality. Yet, I still believed in miracles.

I took the piece of gum that I had been gnawing on far too long out of my mouth, and placed it inside the cap. It would be the seal I needed to keep the bottle dry on the inside. With that done, I was now ready to take a hike up or down the beach. The sand was hard packed and rather easy to walk along.

The previous note stated "Further instructions will be given to you later." I still had not been given any further instructions so I decided I would walk the beach for a very long time. I had looked several times in both directions to see if anyone else was walking the beach, but so far no one could be seen. The sand was still rather hard, but not anything like the tourist town of South Padre Island where cars drove the beach. I did not see any signs of human life here on the beach. No signs of skydivers, surfers, or even horses on the beach- a typical site often found with the invasion of college students every spring break on the island. Today it was simply wildlife… a few birds, shells, grasses, and a lonely jellyfish that had been washed on shore.

As I contemplated my next move, I noticed that the waves were crashing from the north to the south. If I walked north of here and threw my bottle into the water, it would probably end up back here on the shore. That could be disastrous. My choice quickly dwindled to one option.

My other concern that I had not previously considered was the fact that I could be in Mexico. I still wasn't sure of my exact location. The Las Palomas Wildlife reserve south of South Padre Island was as far south as anyone could go before leaving the United States. Walking the beach into Mexico was not an option. The Rio Grande River snaked its way along the southern border of Texas to the Gulf of Mexico, separating the United States from Mexico.

I could still see that there were only three houses to the south and one house to the north. My mind continued to churn. There would be no reason for houses to be built in the state parks if I was truly near the border. My logical thinking had me guessing again to my whereabouts. Since I could see two more houses south of where I currently stood, I thought my chances of seeing anyone would be greater if I headed south. If I were in Mexico, what would the Mexican authorities do to me if they found an American woman walking down the beach without any identity? I wouldn't even be able to explain to them how I got here.

After another attempt to find a logical approach to my decision, I leaned on my instinct. Reasoning kept telling me to head north and forget about my message in the bottle. Time in a small rural jail cell for trespassing could not possibly be as accommodating as the house directly behind me. I'm sure there were other worse case scenarios that I had not thought to explore, but I would not let my mind travel there.

My gut told me to head south. I flung my towel and shoes over my right shoulder and held the bottle in my right hand, hidden beneath the towel. I started walking. The sand between my toes and the warm water were invigorating. As my fear began to subside momentarily, I found enjoyment in the solace that I was experiencing now. My only regret was that I did not carry a bottle of water with me.

I could tell as the sun continued to climb in the sky that the temperature soared a few degrees hotter as well. If I got too hot, I would wade out into the water up to my shorts, or splash some salt water onto my face. I knew I couldn't stay out here for more than an hour or two without becoming crisp.

I decided I would walk as far as the houses, but then turn around and head back. The comfort of my room seemed a little more appealing than I first realized. I had plenty of food, and the luxury of a nice bed and bath. Since I had not received any further instructions, I thought I would hang out down stairs when I returned. Maybe I would sneak around to the front of the house to see what it looks like too. My mind was off on another tangent again.

After I had walked about a mile or so, there was a small alcove with a few rocks at the water's edge. This is where I would place my bottle. It was low tide now, so I would let the waters do their job. At high tide, the bottle would travel wherever the waters would lead.

The sand shifted and became smooth everywhere the water touched it. The waves fifty feet out crashed upon another only to build again and crash a second time before reaching its final doom. Then it retracted and began the journey all over again. The sounds never ended. The waves continued, foaming like cumulus clouds, disappearing only long enough to be covered with a new layer of foam and water. It was mesmerizing.

As I stood observing how different the waves were from yesterday, a white-bellied bird with black legs and beak, and soft charcoal tail feathers scurried in front of me across the receding wet sand with dinner held tightly between both beaks. He was determined not to drop his boon or let any other bird garnish his finding. The bird, charming in every way, was a reminder to me that pleasant things still exist in nature. He was the subtle friend that I needed to see right now.

I walked around two sides of the alcove. I was going to go into the water and look at the other sides, but decided that it really didn't matter. I sat down on one of the rocks for a brief minute, then I noticed a sand dollar half buried in the water. I jumped off the rock to pull it out of the sand. It was about four inches in diameter. I was surprised. I had seen them in tourist shops over the years, but never had I actually seen one on a beach. "Today must be my lucky day," I thought.

I placed my bottle in the water on the south side of the reef exactly where I found the sand dollar. It only stayed there briefly as another wave crashed over the sand. The bottle float-ed momentarily forward onto the beach, and then back again toward the alcove. The waves were crashing here in various directions before falling upon each other, creating my suspicion of an under current.

I turned around to see that the house was about a mile or so down the beach, and it looked to me like the three houses were at least another mile further down the beach. I was still very amused and puzzled. No one had come after me. I was quite a ways from the house now. I could easily run, but that still didn't seem the best choice. The puzzling factor in all of this is that I had been given so much liberty to wander. If the three houses were actually a safe haven for me, they would not allow me to walk there.

As I stood pondering the mind game that I now found myself in, I noticed something moving on the beach near the three houses. It was too far away for me to see, so I waited. Sitting back down on the rock, I watched the figures moving towards me.

Without question, I could see that a man was approach-ing with a dog. I decided to wait just a little longer to see if I could tell whether or not the man was Mexican or American. I was hoping to get another clue to my whereabouts. Before the man was close enough for me to determine his nationality, the dog burst through its invisible wall and raced down the beach as fast as he could run towards me. I don't know if the man told him to go, but it was like a dog breaking through a fence into freedom. The dog was fast approaching.

Then I jumped up and screamed, "Lucy… is that you?" The dog looked identical to Lucy. Maybe I was dreaming, but I thought for sure that the dog coming towards me was Lucy. I shouted again, "Lucy?" She ran even faster.

I stood motionless as my feet sunk into the wet sand as Lucy ran towards me. Her bark was real, and her tail was swaying fast as I got down on my knees to pet her. She almost knocked me over into the sand as she licked my face still panting from her long run. I checked her tag to confirm this wasn't a dream. My Lucy had a caramel color tag with her name printed in capital letters with my phone number.

I closed my eyes and took a deep breath before pulling the tag between the layers of fir. It was my best friend.

By now the man approaching me was running as well, and I could clearly see that it was Cal. I immediately stood up and raced towards him. I flung my arms around him in sheer disbelief as we both grabbed for one another. His embrace and lips, pressed against mine, never felt better than they did right then.

"Cal, you look ravishing," I said as I held his cheeks in the palms of my hands. I then closed my eyes and hugged him as tight as I could. I never wanted to let go. "I can't believe this. I can't believe you're here, Cal," I began rambling.

"Caroline, I missed you so much. I love you, honey. I'm so sorry all of this has happened to you and me."

"I love you too, Cal. I am so glad to see you," I said before kissing him again.

Cal's hair was about four inches longer than it had been when he left home that early morning seven long months ago. He was wearing white shorts with a light blue Polo shirt. He was tan and looked well rested.

"Look at you, Calvin. Long hair just blowing in the breeze," I said looking at him again. "I don't think I have ever seen you with hair this long," I commented.

"Yea, can you believe it? I haven't had many options for a local barber, but I kind of like it. Mr. Boots may have other thoughts," Calvin chuckled.

"I like it too. You definitely have a more relaxed look about yourself," I said as I rubbed my fingers through his hair.

"We have a lot to talk about Caroline. I am so glad we are finally together again. I didn't think we ever would be."

By now, Lucy was rubbing against our legs and continued to wag her tail. "I love you too, Lucy," I said as I reached down to pet her again. "Is one of the bottles for me?" I asked as I picked up a water bottle from the sand. Cal dropped two of them at our feet along with his leather sandals when we first embraced.

"Yes," he said. "I thought you might be thirsty by now."

I took several swallows of water, then poured half the bottle onto Lucy's tongue so she could rehydrate. Cal drank from the other bottle.

"There is so much to say that I don't even know where to

begin," Cal stated as he held my hand. "Let's walk back to the house where you have been staying," he said. "Lunch should be ready for us when we arrive."

"Do you know what's going on?" I asked.

"I do now," Cal said. "I'll tell you everything I know once we get back to the house. How are you dear? I can't imagine what you have gone through this past year."

"I'm fine. It's been difficult, but I'm fine. I actually sold our house and bought a new one in North Valley across from a horse ranch. It's the perfect place for us. I can't wait for you to see it."

"Caroline, there is so much that I don't know about you now, and definitely a lot that you don't know about the situation we encountered. I hate to say it, but we won't be able to go back to Albuquerque. I'm sorry, honey. I truly am," he said as he put his arm around me and hugged me again. "I know it's going to take hours and days for each of us to share what has been going on the past seven and a half months. We'll get through it together this time," he said.

I stopped. "We never get to go back ever?" I asked, still stunned by the news. My feet sunk slowly into the wet sand again as the water rushed past my feet. "Ever? Never? We never get to go back?" I said it again quietly.

I had just spent the past thirty-six hours agonizing over a letter to my parents. It never occurred to me that I could never go home again either. I thought our lives would go back to normal again, if I could only find Cal.

"No honey, we can't. I think you'll understand why once you hear all the details of these strange events. The good news is that we get the house to ourselves for the next four days. The guys will be leaving once our lunch is prepared. They won't be there when we get back. We will have a few days to wrap our minds around all of this."

Calvin continued to hold my hand as we walked in the water up the beach towards the white house. Lucy splashed around, but stayed close to my side the entire hike back. "Has Lucy been with you ever since I was kidnapped?" I asked.

"Yes, she was kidnapped as well, but fortunately the men allowed her to stay with me. That was one of the conditions I agreed upon with them. Lucy was part of the package deal," Cal said without going into further details.

"One of the conditions?" I asked. "Is this something you planned and knew all along? A package deal?" I questioned. Cal could hear the anger and frustration in my voice. My whisper was now a harsh articulation.

"No, it's not like that Caroline," Cal remarked. "I was kidnapped against my will, just like you."

"Then why didn't they- whoever they are- kidnap us both at the same time, if they want us both. Wouldn't that have made it a lot easier on us?" I continued.

"I know you are angry and confused. I was too. Please just trust me and give me time to explain. I don't know everything, but I can try to explain the things that I know," Cal rationalized.

By the time we reached the house, the sand was so hot on the bottom of our feet that we had to run the hundred yards from the water's edge to the house itself. "On your mark, get set, go" I said after I was already ten feet ahead of Cal.

We both sprinted to the French doors where he grabbed me and pressed me against the glass to fondle and kiss me all over again. We were both trying to catch our breaths. "I need a drink, Cal," I said as I pushed him away from me. "I've been out in this heat for nearly two hours, I think."

"I can't wait," he said as he opened the door. He grabbed the plate of chicken croissant sandwiches with fresh grapes and pecans and the bottle of champagne and wine goblets that were left on the kitchen island, while I grabbed for a cold bottle of water that had been on ice along with the bottle of champagne. Pasta salad, chips, and a fresh key lime pie remained on the counter.

Cal ran up the steps, as if we were two teenagers trying to hustle up to a room before being caught, hoping I was following close behind. I stood watching as I relished every swallow of the cold beverage. Lucy had run to the bottom of the stairs following Cal, but abruptly stopped when she realized I wasn't coming. "Caroline," I heard Cal call out in what now seemed like another dream. "Are you coming?" he asked. My mind was spinning. I had fantasized a thousand times of the day when I could have sex again with my husband, never really believing it would ever happen again. And, just moments earlier I would have scurried up the stairs with him, but my mind was hung on the fact that he agreed to let me be kidnapped. I was as anxious as he, until he brought up the word, "conditions."

"Caroline," he pleaded. "Please... he paused. We can talk later. Please just trust me," he said again. Lucy continued to look at me with her big brown eyes while her tail wagged side to side. "I need you now," Cal said with urgency. I wanted him as bad as he wanted me. I just needed to momentarily dismiss the fact that he knew I was being kidnapped. Let it go, I told myself as I dropped the plastic bottle onto the counter. I hurried toward Lucy and patted her on the backside, motioning her to go upstairs. Cal stood waiting, clearly not knowing which direction he should go down the hall. I grabbed a croissant and took a bite as Cal and Lucy followed me to my room. Once inside, Cal shut the door and gently flung me onto the bed as I took a second bite of sandwich causing the croissant to drop onto the floor. He was impatient with my desire to eat first. Amidst a floodgate of emotions, I agreed, being with him couldn't happen soon enough.

Lucy ate the remains of my chicken salad when it fell onto the rug. The answers to all of my questions would have to wait. For now, the only thing that mattered was that Cal was alive and well, and we were together. The heat of his body and the warm moisture of his lips eased my tension. All my worries and concerns began to melt away as he held me tight. I was with my husband again, and I was going to enjoy every moment of our re-acquaintance. Cal was right. Whatever this thing is we were encountering, we would get through it together.

PRELUDE

To the SECOND NOVEL
in the Saying Goodbye SERIES

"Phillip, I tried texting Caroline again but she hasn't answered," Michelle told her husband as their plane began taxiing down the tarmac to the terminal.

"I'm sure Caroline is waiting for us out front just like we had planned," Phillip responded back to his new bride, giving her a kiss on the cheek. "Your cell service is probably just acting up since your phone was shut off for the past eight days."

They could faintly hear the airline attendant announce over the intercom, "Please remain in your seats until the aircraft has come to a complete stop. We will be taxiing for another minute before arriving at Gate B9 in Terminal 3 at the B Concourse. You may turn on your cell phones now. We appreciate you choosing to travel with us today. We look forward to serving you again."

The newlyweds were returning from their honeymoon in Maui where they stayed at the Hyatt in Lahaina. It was the perfect getaway. They had just the right amount of leisure, fun in the sun, island dining, and the things honeymooners do best.

"Phillip, her phone is ringing," Michelle continued after he grabbed their carry-on luggage from the bin above their heads. "She's not even responding to my phone call," Michelle added.

The couple, who had been seated near the front of the plane, filed in line to exit the Boeing 747. Not only in a few short minutes would they be stepping over the threshold of the plane onto the jet bridge, but they would also be stepping back into reality as a newly married couple.

"Thank you for flying with us," the attendant said once again as they exited the plane. Michelle, oblivious to the remark, kept walking forward looking down at her phone. "Thank you," Phillip responded back flashing a quick smile to the attendant.

"Quinn," Phillip teased, "put your phone away, while we wait for our luggage to unload. I'm sure Caroline is waiting for us. Phillip then grabbed Michelle's hand as he escorted her through the airport to the baggage terminal.

"You're right. I'm sure she's waiting in her Jeep out front just like we had planned," Michelle reassured herself. "And, if she's not here yet, we can always grab a bite to eat. I'm hungry."

"Yea, I am too now that you mention it," Phillip agreed. Several more minutes went by as they waited with other passengers to retrieve their luggage. Phillip had a typical black suitcase that could have been claimed by any number of people. Michelle, in her lust for life, did not want her luggage to go unnoticed. She sported a bright orange hard cover suitcase.

The carousel turned on and began rotating when several black suitcases launched forward shooting down the ramp. Within a minute Michelle's suitcase came sliding down too. There was no doubt at all to the rightful owner of that suitcase. Large and bold in the center were the initials MQ. Everyone standing there knew that suitcase did not belong to them.

"Well, that's easy enough to spot," Phillip told his wife as he winked. He took it off the carousel as he continued to look for his own suitcase. "Where did you even find a suitcase like this one?" he asked.

"It only took losing my luggage once for me to decide to make a change. I had traveled to Tennessee a few summers ago for a teacher's conference, and when I arrived my luggage was nowhere to be found. The airline literally lost my suitcase. My black suitcase, just like the one you use, was gone."

"Maybe someone mistook it for their suitcase," Phillip reasoned.

"Maybe, but the bottom line is that I was without my clothes. The airline said it would show up, but to this day I have never seen it again."

"Really?" Philip responded.

"Before even checking into my hotel, I drove straight to the mall to pick up a few things that I would need. When I walked by a luggage store, the bright orange one stood out like a sore thumb. I immediately knew that was the right suitcase for me. I haven't had any problems since. See, I have my suitcase, but you are still looking for yours," Michelle responded in a haughty, but lovable tone of voice. "I don't think anyone will walk away with this one."

"Point well taken," Phillip remarked still looking for his suitcase that already had circled the carousel. "Awe, there it is," he said, as it turned the corner at the opposite end from where they were standing. After waiting a few more seconds for it to arrive, he said, "Let's go look for Caroline."

The couple, still gleaming with the unspoken glow of being newly wed, towed their suitcases out of the baggage claim area to the front doors. They scanned the pickup and drop off zone without any signs of Caroline or her Jeep. "Try her again," Phillip stated. "Surely, she must be around here somewhere. We have been off the plane thirty minutes already.

"I'm getting a bit nervous now, Phillip. She's not answering her phone yet." Michelle was puzzled. "She had all of our flight information, and I specifically said that I would call when the plane arrived. Forgetting about us isn't something Caroline would do."

"Yea, it doesn't seem like she's the type of person who would not show up," Phillip agreed. "Well, let's go to short term parking to see if we can find her Jeep. Maybe she came early and decided to park."

The couple followed the signs up the escalator through another corridor to the short-term parking. A blast of warm air rushed over them as they walked through the doors. "Back to the fresh, clear air of New Mexico," Phillip said. "It just smells like home here."

"The air is definitely crisp here," Michelle added. "Good thing she drives a Jeep," Michelle responded as they began to canvass the hundreds of vehicles in front of them. "At least it should be easy to see." Sure enough, Michelle was right. It was easy to spot a Jeep in the parking lot. It was even easier to spot a red Jeep in the parking lot. As far as Michelle could see, there were none.

"It looks like we are down to one, Michelle," Phillip responded. "I see five of them from here. A yellow one parked over there, as he pointed to the left of where they were standing. A black one over there, and a gray one a few spots down. Way over there is another dark one, "Phillip continued as he pointed to the right of where they were walking. And, I think there is one down that far aisle," he said.

"Where?" Michelle asked. "I can only see four of them."

Phillip put his luggage down, and placed his hands on the back of Michelle's hips.

"What are you doing, Phillip?" Michelle screeched as he lifted her six inches off the ground.

"I'm adding a few inches to your height so you can see better," he said. "Can you see it now?"

Michelle instantly lost her composure as she began laughing. Phillip then turned her around and kissed her. "You honestly thought you were going to help me see better?" she joked as she held him close to her.

"No, but I thought I might get you to laugh," he said. "I see a red, or as Caroline might say, a scarlet Jeep, but I don't think it belongs to Caroline."

"How do you know if it is way down yonder, and we are still way up here?" Michelle questioned.

"I don't think it has a bike rack," Phillip answered.

"Oh, so you were trying to get me to laugh because you knew I would be uptight if I saw a red Jeep that didn't belong to Caroline?" she asked.

"Yes. Did it work?" Phillip continued.

"Considering that you haven't known me for a long time, you nailed it. So, now what?" she asked.

"Why don't you stay here for a minute while I quickly walk down to confirm that the Jeep does not belong to Caroline," Phillip said as he rushed towards the vehicle. In no time he was back. "No, it's not hers. It has a baby seat in the back. Let's check out front one more time, and call her again. If we still can't find her, we can take a cab home."

Phillip and Michelle looked several more times, but could not find their friend. "You probably should leave a text message that we are taking a taxi home, just in case she decides to come for us," Phillip suggested. He then flagged for the cab as they approached the curb.

"Do you feel like making dinner tonight?" Phillip asked after they got into the cab.

"Not really, do you?" Michelle asked in return.

"No," Phillip agreed. "Can you head towards the fast food restaurants on Gibson Boulevard?" he then asked the driver. "I'll give your specific directions from there to our home," he added. "First, we need to grab a quick bite of food."

By the time they reached their house, they already had devised a plan to search for Caroline. They took their suitcases inside, used the bathroom, and Michelle checked her emails in hopes that she had received a message from Caroline.

"This can't be happening," Michelle told Phillip as they hopped into her car to head over to Caroline's house.

"Don't panic yet", Phillip said, trying to calm Michelle's spirits.

"It's deja vu all over again," Michelle whimpered.

"Let's hope not, Michelle. Let's hope not," he said again trying to reassure him self this time. "I'm sure glad that it's only six o'clock right now rather than ten o'clock. At least we have a few daylight hours in front of us.

When they arrived at Caroline's house, Michelle shuffled through her purse to find the house key. Caroline had finally given her one after she had all the locks changed. Phillip knocked on the door, but there was no response. Michelle unlocked the door and they walked inside. Lucy was not there to greet them, nor was Caroline.

"You look inside and I'll look outside," Phillip immediately said as he ran to the backyard to check the pool. He dreaded what he might find, but knew that he had to look. The last thing he wanted was for his new bride to find her best friend out there.

He had a sigh of relief to find the pool empty. "That's a relief," he said to himself as he reentered the house. "She's not outside," he told Michelle as he walked down the hallway towards Caroline's bedroom.

"I don't see anything out of place in her bedroom," Michelle responded. "I definitely don't think there has been a robbery either. The house is neat and clean as always," she added. After searching the entire house, they walked into the garage to find her Jeep and her mountain bike missing.

"She must have gone on a trail ride today," Michelle remarked. "Let me call Josh and Jason to see if they know anything."

Phillip continued to snoop around while Michelle made the phone calls. He even tried to get onto her computer, but couldn't decipher her password. Everything looked in orderly fashion to him.

"Joshua didn't answer his phone so I left a text message. Jason said that they all rode at Ponderosa Trail this morning. He thought Caroline was planning to come, but she never showed up. He said that he didn't think much of it since her riding schedule has been so infrequent the past several months."

"Well, should we head out there now to see if she made it out there?" Phillip asked.

"If we go, we probably need to get some of the guys to go with us," Michelle said. "By the time we get out there, we will probably only have about one hour of daylight. It's a very scenic trail with woods, water, a ravine, and cliffs. If she was riding the trail alone and something happened, then it would take a while for her to get help. It will take longer than an hour to search that trail. And, that's assuming that she went to that trail and rode it today."

"Is there anyone else you can call who might know what her plans were for the day?" Phillip then asked.

"Felicia might know. She's Caroline's best friend from work. She's the friend who answered the phone that first night when you called me trying to invite yourself to our party," Michelle reminded her husband.

"Oh, she's the one who told me that there wasn't a Quinn around?" he asked.

Squirming, Michelle replied "Yep, she's the one. Matter of fact, I was right here, lying on Caroline's bed when I called you back," Michelle said.

"Well, you better call her now," Phillip said as he tossed his wife down onto the bed. Quinn wouldn't want to miss another important phone call."

Phillip began to caress his wife while Michelle tried to make the phone call.

"Stop it, Phillip," Michelle said as the phone began to ring.

"Just one kiss, Quinn. Just one kiss," he insisted. By now Phillip couldn't keep his hands off Michelle.

"Felicia?" Michelle inquired when the familiar voice answered the phone.

"Yes," she replied.

"This is Michelle. Michelle Stratton," she said before being nudged in the leg by Phillip. "Terric. This is Michelle Terric, Michelle said trying to correct herself. "You know who I am. I'm Caroline Richard's friend. I haven't actually had to say my new last name since the wedding, so I'm still working on that."

"Oh, no problem at all, Michelle. I know who you are and I completely understand," Felicia commented. "What can I do for you tonight? Aren't you just getting back from your honeymoon?" she then asked.

Phillip finally settled down enough to let me talk uninterrupted.

"Yes. Yes. We just got back about an hour and a half ago, and that's the problem. Caroline was supposed to pick us up from the airport, but she never showed. I have called and texted countless times with no response. Phillip and I are actually at her house now, and she is not here. Both her and Lucy are gone. She must have gone somewhere with her Jeep and her mountain bike. I am calling to see if you might know what her plans were for today or this weekend."

There was a moment of silence on the other end of the line.

"Felicia?" Michelle asked again. "Are you still there?"

"Yes. I'm sorry Michelle. I'm just kind of… I guess I'm surprised. It's completely unlike Caroline to fall back on her word. She would never leave anyone stranded."

"We are fine, but I'm concerned about Caroline. Did she say anything at all to you about her plans today?" Michelle asked again. "Jason told us that the biking club was going to ride at Ponderosa Trail this morning. Did she say anything to you about riding there? Apparently, the guys thought she was coming, but she never showed.

"She said that she might go there. She wasn't sure. She mostly talked about picking you up at the airport. She was really excited that you would be coming home on a Saturday rather than a Sunday. She said she would be able to talk with you before going to work on Monday. I think she was even planning to have you over for brunch on Sunday morning," Felicia said. "She figured you wouldn't have time to go grocery shopping so that was one thing she could do to help."

"Gracias, Felicia. I think Ponderosa Trail is the place we need to start," Michelle remarked.

"I'm not sure if there is much I can do to help with three young children at my side other than make phone calls here from the house, but if there is anything at all you need, please let me know. Adios amigos," Felecia said.

"Un poco de español es bueno para el alma," Phillip piped in.

"What?" Michelle asked as her husband began caressing her again.

"A little Spanish is good for the soul, my wife. A little Spanish is good for the soul. Now kiss me. We have a lot of

227

work ahead of us," he claimed.

SAYING GOODBYE

is the first book of the

Saying Goodbye Collection

Sheree Publishing

ACKNOWLEDGEMENT

Life reminds me of the many roads I have traveled. Some are packed with dirt, gravel, potholes, and detours. Some are frehsly paved and scenic, while others are an uphill climb.

I wish to thank my parents and family who have always been supportive of my dreams. I didn't get here alone as no one ever does. Michelle McSorley was instrumental as I began this journey. Julianne Meyer has been an amazing prayer warrior. Susan Crites and Kathy DeHaan have walked with me every step of the way, lifting me up when I have fallen, assisting in every way imaginable, and praying for me unselfishly. From the botton of my heart, I want to thank you all.

Most importantly, I want to thank God for graciously giving my daughter additional days and years to become the beautiful young woman that she has become. He saved her from death multiple times over during the summer of 2016. It is through his mercy and love that she lives. I am forever grateful to him for protecting her.

Shelli Sheree has traveled throughout all 48 continental states and Hawaii, with Alaska being the only state left for her to visit. In 1985, she traveled over 10,000 miles around the perimeter of the United State by bicycle, and then traveled throughout Europe two years later again on bike. As a hockey mom, she has traveled throughout the Midwest and Canada. She loves the Caribbean beaches and white sands of South Florida. More than traveling, she loves to write. Shelli is married and has three grown children.